A Vampire's Dream

FATE'S CHRONICLES
BOOK THREE

RHIANNON FUTCH

For my daughters.
I couldn't have made it here without you.
I love you so much.

Contents

One

NATASHA

"This book is useless! I can't find anything that will help us find her in here, and the search function doesn't damn work for me!" Ajah snickers as I slam my hands down on the book. This does not help my mood at all. "What are you laughing at?"

The tiger shifter twists her mouth up on one side, completely unafraid of me she says, "I would be surprised if it worked the same for you. You aren't the Chronicler, I would bet it wouldn't work if you went and told a family that they weren't holding up their end of the contract either. You're just going to have to look through the book the old-fashioned way - one page at a time."

She out right laughs as I groan and let my head fall

onto the book in front of me. As her laughter dies down, Ajah tells me, "You know, if I were a witch there is a good probability that I wouldn't put my really good spells into a book meant for preserving the legacy. I would keep those to myself. However, the book your Grams sent over, that was a personal book that someone kept until they died. I think it is more likely you will find what you are looking for in that book."

By the time she finishes speaking, I am staring at her open-mouthed. How did this not occur to me? "You are exactly right. It is much more likely that the contributors to this book were like the Hales, and the lead bitch would definitely hold back on things. Wait here, I am going to switch out the books." Ajah nods and leans back in her chair as I leave the room. I can feel her watching my hips sway as I walk, but there is no threat in her gaze, only admiration. Honestly, I mind her polite gaze much less than the stares of the creeps out in public. These stairs are so much nicer now that I am a vampire. I think I could literally run up them in my heels, but I need not be anywhere that fast.

Walking into the office I shared with Fate until her disappearance, the pain hits all over again. I feel my throat closing and I can see Fate's resignation, all of us watching helplessly as Charles takes her away. Shaking my head to clear it, I go after the book I came here to get.

An hour of paging through this book later, we have to face facts. We will not find a spell in the books we have available to bring back our Fate. I close the book and Ajah looks up, "Can't you just write a spell to find her?"

I make a face as I repeat her words back to her, "No! I can't just write a spell! It takes skill and knowledge of how spells work to do that. This is why I don't have my own spell book. I'd rather just set a fool on fire than deal with him if he can't act right." Getting up to pace, I continue, "You know, you may have something there. When I don't have the right spell for the job I usually go see Grams. Maybe that is what we need to do now! Yes! I need to go see Grams. Would you like to go with? I need to find Billy, he has been eager to meet her. This isn't the best time, but who knows when that will be?"

Ajah nods and says, "I'll get the suburban out and we can take Owen. I know you don't need protection, but it makes us happy. Go find your man." She leaves the kitchen with me staring after her this time. I guess the bodyguards probably are bored as hell. Shrugging to myself, I grab the book and take it back to the office before heading down the hall to Devon's office. They are usually holed up in there.

I tap on the door, and it swings open. It wasn't closed fully so even a little tap made it swing open, Devon and Billy look over at me from either side of his massive desk. They have papers strewn everywhere. This office is a nightmare right now. I carefully pick my way through discarded papers and stop a foot or so from the end of the desk. "Hello gentlemen. We seem to have run into a stumbling block as there are no spells in the books we currently have that will suit our needs. However," I hold up a hand to stop Devon before he starts talking, "I think my Grams may have one that will work. Or, she may be able to write one. Before you ask, no, I cannot. It's a sore spot, don't ask."

Devon nods, "I understand. I know you will do everything in your power to find her. As will I. Are you leaving now?"

"Yes. Actually, I came to see if Billy wanted to go with me since he wants to meet Grams and it seems like the right time is likely to be half past never, I figured may as well poke the cat now. So, do you want to go?"

I look to Billy, he is smiling wide as he says, "I thought you would never ask. Yes, let's go meet your wonderful Grams."

Devon watches as Billy stands and comes to put an arm around me and pull me a little closer. Devon looks away, blinking fast. Clearing his throat, he says, "Be safe, I'll see you when you get back." He is gone before we can respond, Billy looks toward the door and says, "He isn't handling this very well. Having her so close and knowing that Charles has her, well, it messes with his head."

We head out to the truck, his hand in mine as he continues, "I can't imagine what kind of hell he has gone through every time she was snatched away from him. You and I, we love each other, but if we split up for whatever reason, it won't hurt the other one anywhere near how it has hurt him every single time. Usually she is dead, but this time she is here in this city. And he only just found her, I can't even imagine how he is managing right now."

Billy talks all the way to the truck and I realize we got there much faster than I would have before I was turned. I would have definitely done this a lot sooner if they had assured me that I would have a dear friend to spend the long years with. I love every aspect of being a vampire, and I thought I wouldn't like the blood-drinking aspect. As it turns out, that isn't so bad. It really is just another food source. Kind of like eating meat. The blood we drink doesn't even have to be human, any blood will work.

Getting in the truck I tell Ajah the address to Grams' place and she pops it into the gps. Billy closes the door after climbing in behind me and off to grandmother's house we go.

Arriving at Gram's house always brings me a sense of peace. I think she designed it that way, or perhaps ensured it would be by casting a spell on the place. She does see all sorts of people and the rule at her place has ever been that whatever troubles follow you are left at the end of the drive. I only ever remember her having to enforce that rule once. A wolf and a vampire were in love with the same person, and the wolf showed up at Grams for healing and Grams therapy. The vampire followed him to Gram's place and after she let him in; the vampire tried to attack the wolf. The wolf tried shouting 'Not here!' but the vampire paid it no mind. Then Grams clapped once.

The sound was amplified, and it rang through the house. The wolf and vampire were both frozen in place. It looked massively uncomfortable. The wolf had his hands out, pressed against the vampire's chest to keep him back while the vampire had buried his long nails into the wolf's shoulders. I watched as Grams plucked the fingers of the vampire out of the wolf. The wolf whimpered with each one. She pushed the vampire over to the corner, faced him into it and told him that he could stay there until he learned some manners. He actually threatened to eat her once he got free, but she laughed at him. Told him that all he would accomplish was an acute case of tooth loss.

She eventually sorted the two of them out, and the vampire became a great friend of hers. The girl they were both after was human and wasn't interested in either of them once she found out they were not human.

I lead the way to the door. All the scents are distracting for everyone but me. I have been here so many times that even with my enhanced sense of smell, it just smells like home. Grams is at the door by the time we get to it, beaming and saying, "Oh! You brought your young man! And some new friends! How wonderful! Where is my Fate at? I want to see her too. Could she not make it?"

I freeze, remembering that I haven't told Grams yet. "That is what we came to talk to you about Grams, Fate is missing. We know who took her but not where, and we need your help."

She puts her hand over her heart, "Oh child, I so hoped that dream had been a lie. Well, come in, come in. All of you. Let's get some brandy-laced tea and you'll tell me all of it."

We file in, Owen being last in, shuts the door. Grams kitchen has always magically managed to accommodate however many people showed up and needed a seat, today was no exception. Last time I had been here, the kitchen was cozy with a small table and three chairs. Today the kitchen was massive and the table equally so. It was now rectangular and had six chairs, one at either end and two on each side. "Sit down, sit down. I'll get the tea, you all get comfortable."

Grams is ever Grams, and she is always about her tea. Usually it is an herbal blend suited for the situation, but today I have a feeling it will be dark and laced with cacao, sweetened with caramel and dosed heavily with brandy. Grams has always said that heavy things need heavy teas. The longer I live, the more I think she is right about everything.

Finally she brings a tray over to the table, passing cups all around. Once she has settled, she looks expectantly at all of us and sips her tea. I grin and lift my cup. The fragrance is divine. I was right, cacao with caramel and brandy. Everyone else follows my lead and sighs of enjoyment, along with compliments to Grams echo through the kitchen. She smiles graciously and thanks everyone before turning to me, "Now. Tell me what happened to our Fate."

I tell her the whole sorry story, from beginning to end.

By the end, she has tears in her eyes. I go on to tell her that we have been searching for a spell to find her.

"I think I can help you with that, but it will take a minute for me to go through the books and find the right one. If our Fate doesn't come back safe, I will curse the pants right off that boy. She is family, I look at her as my other granddaughter. It would break my heart to lose either one of you." She sniffs and focuses on Billy, "Now, cheer me up. Tell me how this one won your heart in such a short time? I bet he kissed it right out of you. He looks like a kisser."

Billy is grinning from ear to ear at this point while I am lit up like a damn stop light. He stands and walks over to kneel next to Grams chair, taking her hand he places a very light kiss on her knuckles, "I am Billy Webb. I come from a distinguished line of chiefs whose tribe is long extinct. I have spent more time in Ireland than Africa, because I never could bear to watch my people pass from this world or see the disgust on their faces when they recognized me for what I am. I see where Natasha has inherited her beauty from. You are lovely as a spring day." He kisses her knuckles once more and returns to the seat beside me while Grams fans herself.

"Now I am very curious about your young vampire lover. Is it it warm in here? Goodness…"

I laugh, "We met because he is Devon's friend and came to help Devon protect Fate."

Grams raises her brows, "Two vampires, multiple shifters, a fire witch, and she is an air witch but he still took her? I don't understand how it is that Devon has not taken care of this problem during one of the times she was dead?"

Billy clears his throat, "I think I can help with that. I recently found out that Devon's sire, also the man that took Fate, did not tend to his duties as sire. Devon, thanks to popular media, was under the impression that killing Charles would kill him as well. So he has held off all this time. Cursing himself as selfish for not being willing to die because he wanted to see Fate again."

Grams has a hand over her mouth, "Oh my, how horrible for him and her both. Did she know? Does she know?"

I nod, "She does now. She did not know until recently. She was the one to pry the information out of Devon and the one to find the vampire code in the chronicle. After that she put two and two together, forcing Devon to talk to Billy. Billy is training Devon now. So these mistakes will not happen again."

Grams is deep in thought, staring down into her cup. We can feel the magic in the air, I don't know what she is doing, but she is definitely doing something, so we wait. When Grams finally looks up from her cup, she says, "I don't think he could have killed him. Someone else is pulling strings in this game. Though I am given permission to help you find her, I was also warned that there would be dire consequences for Fate if Charles dies. Whatever you do, do not kill him."

"What? Don't kill him? Grams, he has murdered her over and over again. It isn't safe to leave him alive!"

"I know, I know. This is what I was told," she looks each of us in the eye, "if he dies the repercussions for Fate will be bad. He is meant to play a part in her life. I don't know what part that is, I'm guessing it isn't murderer. Maybe our string puller will eventually see fit to reveal the whole story. Either way, don't kill Charles. No matter what! He has to live or I get the feeling that Fate may get taken out of the rebirth cycle."

I gasp, "What? How is that even possible?"

"I don't know. I don't know for sure that I am right about this, it is just a feeling I get. Now I am tired. You all should go, I will search for the spell after my nap. I don't think we have to be in too big a hurry to find Fate, anyway. Not now. Give me a hug before you go." I take my empty cup and set it in the sink. Everyone else follows my example. I hug Grams and she whispers to me, "Don't worry, she will be fine." I step away and everyone stands there until Grams says, "She isn't the only one I require hugs from before you leave." Billy walks over with a smile and kneels down to hug her. With my vampire hearing, I can hear her tell him, "Don't let her worry so much. It will work out."

She hugs Ajah next, "You're going to meet her very soon, relax. It will be fun." Owen is last in line and to him she says, "Dear boy, it is all going to get better. Just you watch."

We file out as Grams heads off to her bed. With as

much magic as she spent this afternoon, I wouldn't be surprised if she slept till morning. On the way home Billy asks, "Did I tell you the twins should be here tomorrow?"

"No, Ajah, Owen, did he tell either of you?"

They shake their heads no, and Billy flushes a bit. "Sorry, I forget sometimes that I need to share information. Ryna and Seamus will arrive sometime tomorrow morning."

Ajah says, "I will make sure Steve knows. I think he is due to be on duty for the door in the morning."

"Thanks, Ajah. What are the twins like Billy?"

"Seamus is short and kind of stocky. He is pale, so white he gleams. He has red hair and lives to annoy Ryna. He can speak just about any language ever spoken within minutes of having heard it spoken. Ryna is tiny. She has golden hair and skin. She is very feminine in her dress with a heavy dose of goth. Her humor is dark and snarky. When she gets icily polite, she is mad. Dangerous mad. She gets her jollies telling Seamus how he should dress and by hunting down murderers and rapists."

"Well, there are worse ways to pass the time, I suppose."

Two

My coffee is only a couple of sips old when we hear the door. Steve leaves the kitchen to answer the door while Natasha and Billy stay and work on their coffee. Minutes later Steve leads the palest man I have ever seen into the kitchen. His smile is wide as he circles the island to greet Billy. Standing in the recently vacated doorway is a tiny, golden goddess. She is wearing a black dress A-line dress that stops mid thigh and has a wide white collar. Patent leather heels on her feet and her long hair flowing loosely down her back do everything to complete the goth but very feminine look. I think I'm in lust. Behave Ajah! This is the best job you have ever had, do not fuck it up!

I will myself under control, though Steve smirks a little

because he can smell the pheromones my excitement caused. He winks to let me know he isn't going to say anything to clue in anyone else and I tip my head slightly in thanks. I tune back into the conversation just in time for Billy to start the introductions. He introduces Natasha first, then me, then Steve. I say hello to both of them, but my eyes can't help drifting over to watch Ryna. She draws me like a moth to a flame. Mother Moon, how am I going to stay away from her? Oh no, she is going to be training us! I am going to die and it will be my own fault for not paying attention. Shit!

"Ajah? Ajah? Earth to Ajah? Hello?"

I realize a hand is waving in front of me and they have called my name repeatedly. This is so embarrassing. Maybe I can play it off like I am not fully awake yet? "Sorry, I was off in my own little world. What's up?"

Billy says, "Ryna is happy to train everyone here, and we were trying to figure out when and where."

"Well, we are kind of here unless one of you needs to go out. So pretty much anytime. As for where, there is a giant basement with reinforced walls. I think that might do, unless you have a better idea, Natasha?"

Oh, thank goodness. The attention is back on someone else. Excellent, they decided on the basement and later this afternoon. Great. "Ok, well, it is nice meeting you all. I am going to go have a shower now, finish waking up." I take my cup and all but run out of the kitchen and down the hall to my own room.

Natasha

I haven't seen Ajah act like she was scared of something ever. Even when we were getting shot at, she was amazing. Caution aplenty, but no fear. She just ran out like her tail was on fire. I notice that Ryna is watching the doorway Ajah just ran through with something akin to hunger. Oooh, I think Ryna is hot for our Ajah and if her behavior is anything to go by, Ajah may be just as hot for her. Oh, this could be glorious.

Billy asks me, "Have we got rooms set up for Seamus and Ryna?"

"We do, would you like to visit your rooms now and maybe get a nap in before we do our training this afternoon?"

Seamus answers before Ryna can open her mouth, "Yes, that would be lovely."

"Perhaps my dear brother will see his way clear to clothes that have been more recently acquainted with a wash."

I laugh as I grab my coffee and lead the way.

Just as I get back to the kitchen my phone rings, Billy gives it a look and tells me, "It's Maggie."

I rush over to answer the phone, "Hi Maggie, what can I do for you?"

"Hi Natasha! I can't seem to get in touch with Fate, but she asked me to find something for her and I think I found just the right place. Do you know where she is?"

"Oh shit, Maggie, I am so sorry I haven't been in touch with you. Fate has been kidnapped by Charles. We've been working hard to find out where she is being held. Honestly, I forgot to tell my Grams."

"Oh no! Is she ok? I mean, you don't sound like he is going to injure her?"

"Well, I don't feel like he is. It seemed like his entire plan is to keep her locked up with him until she falls in love with him. I guess he read up on Stockholm syndrome? So what did Fate have you searching for?"

"Devon can't hear us, can he?"

"No, Billy can, but he won't say anything if I ask him not to or I could leave the room."

"No, no, Billy is fine. This is meant to be a surprise for Devon. Fate decided to buy a house for everyone to fit in. She said with you guys and bodyguards and the twins coming and the elder, she wanted everyone to be comfortable without breaking the time-space continuum putting more and more spaces in a finite area."

"Oh, and you found a place? Is it gorgeous? Tell me about it."

"It has been on the market for a few years. It is well kept and worth the price."

"What's wrong with it? There are plenty of rich jerks looking for a showpiece, what's the catch?"

"It's haunted. The woman that built it is haunting the

place. According to the owners who have moved to Hawaii, the house won't be livable if the ghost doesn't approve the buyer first. So far, everyone that has gone in there has come running back out screaming bloody murder. The agent only told me about it because he hates going out there. He says he has seen the ghost every time, and it freaks him out. I asked if she was doing anything strange. He said quote, 'It's a fucking ghost floating through the house. What isn't strange about that?' End quote. The agent is not part of the community. Chances are, none of the people he took out there are part of the community either. I think it could be perfect for you all, and I think it is likely the ghost will approve of people that don't get frightened because she entered the room. I know it will keep until you get Fate back."

"No. I want to see it. Fate was adamant before she left that I keep her plans moving. Send me the listing and I'll have a look to decide whether or not it would be worth going to look. And interview with the ghost. Ha."

"Sure thing. I will email it now. Give me a call or text me with whatever you decide so I know whether I should keep looking."

"Sounds great, thank you, bye!"

"Bye!"

I look over at Billy, "My heart is breaking for Fate. Did you hear both sides of that?"

"I did. She was planning to surprise him with a house that will fit the masses. Well, if this house is a fit, it will be waiting for her to get back."

Three

CHARLES

I can't believe I have her here with me. I want to spend all my time with her. I know I can't push too fast, she barely knows me beyond being the guy that has been murdering her all this time. Oh well, at least with her being a vampire now I will have plenty of time to help her see that she is meant for me and I am meant for her. Ah Gods, the taste of her is enough to drive a man wild. It took all I had to stop drinking from her.

"Sir, there is a woman at the door. She claims she is your mother?"

"She what?" I stand up from my chair, placing my hands on the desk in front of me, "You're joking, aren't you? It is in poor taste my man, but I'll let it slide this time."

"No, sir. I am not joking at all. There is a woman at the door swearing that she is your mother and she is adamant that you be brought out or she be let in."

Scrunching my face I say, "Really?" Walking around the desk, I head toward the front door, curious to find out who would try to pass themselves off as my mother. I get to the entry and see three of my guards standing in front of Fate's sister? What? Either she plans something stupid or she has lost her mind. Stopping the guard next to me, I tell him, "That is Fate's sister. Check the perimeter and the house for anyone else."

As I draw near my guards part so that Pru can see me, she squeals in delight and says, "Oh my sweet boy! I have missed you so!" She tries to run to me, but the guards stop her, grabbing her arms and holding her up in the air.

I stay well out of her reach. It is strange, but she sounds like my mother. My mother used to call me her sweet boy too. What is going on here? Fate didn't tell me that mental illness ran in her family, but this woman is steady stepping like she is going to get somewhere, though her feet are not touching the ground.

"Hello Pru. Are you feeling well currently?"

"Oh yes, I am feeling better than ever. I have all of my memories back now, just like Fate does. You still look like you did when you were a little, your eyes have changed, but I can still see my sweet boy in that face. I know you don't believe me yet, but I am your mother here in this new body. And! I got myself turned earlier, I am a vampire now, just like you! We will have all the time in the world to catch up. I want to know everything about you!"

"Hmm, I think it will be safe to set her down." Pru immediately runs over to hug me, but I hold a hand out to stop her from engaging. Something is wildly off with Pru and I don't know what. I need to talk to Fate. "Well, Pru, I have a sitting room over here. I would like for you to make yourself comfortable in there while I finish a few things."

She seems pouty about it but agrees, "Don't worry, sweet boy, I understand. It will take some adjustment since you have been without your mom for so very long." I watch with my mouth hanging open as she wanders off into the sitting room I pointed at. Turning to my guards, I start to give them instructions when there is another knock at the door. What the hell? No one is supposed to know where I live and yet, in the space of fifteen minutes, I have two different visitors. One of the guards answers the door. Of course. My actual father is here. Apparently I am going to be paying for all my sins now.

"Let him in. Father, so nice to see you after all this time. To what do I owe the pleasure of your presence?"

"It occurred to me fifty years or so ago that I should maybe talk to you about some things that happened."

Pru steps into the doorway of the sitting room, "You! I would recognize that voice anywhere, Judson Armstrong! How dare you!"

Two of my guards intercept Pru as she runs toward my father with her hands in front of her like claws. Judson's eyes get big like saucers, "How the fuck did your mother find you?" He asks as Pru spews profanities and screams about everything being his fault. I shrug, "I have no idea how either of you found me. But here you both are showing up within minutes of each other."

"I don't think she has all her marbles still." He is watching her like the train wreck you just can't look away from, no matter how horrifying it is.

"You might be right about that. However, as you seem to agitate her condition greatly, can we perhaps meet a different time to discuss whatever you need to talk about? It has kept this long, I don't imagine it will go stale if we wait another day or three."

Judson nods, "Of course. Um, how about we meet at the O'Kierks bar tomorrow? Say around one?"

"Yes, that sounds great, now if you'll excuse me…"

"Oh, yes, yes."

My father turns and rushes out of the front door, the guard shutting and locking it behind him. As soon as he is gone, Pru calms down and says to me, "Stay away from him, sweet boy. He is nothing but trouble." Then she turns and goes into the sitting room. I don't even know what to think at this point. Before I head off to find Fate I motion to the guards that were holding Pru to stand guard at the door of the sitting room. They nod and take up positions on either side of the door. I head up the stairs and knock on Fate's door. No answer, so I open it and pop my head in, but I don't see her sleeping either. I head back downstairs, checking the garden, kitchen, dining areas, until I find her in the library.

I knock gently on the door; I don't want to startle her. When she looks up from her book, I walk in and sit down across from her, "I have some very strange news." She nods her head for me to go on, "Your sister is here and she is claiming to be my mother." The expressions that flit across Fate's face are almost comical. Surprise, fear, anger, and then shock. The fear and anger are the ones that are very curious to me. But not the point right now. "Do you have any idea what she is doing here or how she found this place?"

She shakes her head no, saying, "I don't have the slightest idea. I can tell you that recently she has been pretty far off her rocker and that she is very mad at me right now. We have had a falling out recently. It might be better if she doesn't know that I am here at all. I think I am going to take my book and go hole up in my room. You do not want that level of screech in your house, I assure you. It hurt my ears then and I can't imagine it is any better with vampire hearing. I bid you adieu."

With her goodbye, Fate is up and gone from the room before I can ask even one more question. I wonder what they had a falling out over? Why would Fate take off to her room instead of trying to go see her sister, even if they had an argument? There must be more to the story. I have to find out what is up with Pru. I guess to start with I better go talk to the horse herself. Damn it.

Pru jumps up as soon as I step in the door of the sitting

room, her excitement as visible as that of a small child. She runs over and reaches up to hug me, "I am so happy to have found you again. I am never going away from you, ever. What have you been doing all this time? Have you been well? Has your mangy father been around the entire time? We might have to put a stop to that. He is not good for my boy, no no."

Carefully extricating myself from her arms, I take a step back, "Let's sit down and have a talk, Pru. I think we should get reacquainted." I wait for her to sit and take a chair across from her, "First, are you aware that your sister is my prisoner?" The change in her demeanor is instantaneous. She went from happy and adoring to vicious and hateful without even a blink.

"What do you mean she is *here*? *That bitch* should be in the *ground*! She is vile and hateful and horrible! Why would you have her here? How could you! You're with her, aren't you?"

I sit back in my chair, "Pru, I am going to need you to calm down and sit down. Do you understand?"

She looks around like she has just realized what she did and sits, folding her hands in her lap, the picture of repentance. "I'm sorry, my darling boy. I didn't mean to get so worked up. My sister and I have had a falling out recently, I am sure you didn't even know. She is supremely duplicitous and would not tell you about all the dirty tricks she pulled all her life."

Hmm, that does not ring true. Not from her mouth, nor from the checking into Fate I did. Fate isn't a mean person.

She is the nicest person I have met, as far as I can find. When she came into money, she started hiring friends and trying to do good things for the magical community. I wonder what Pru is hiding. "Really? I would never have guessed. Tell me more."

"Oh no, I don't want to talk about her, it just makes me angry. And I have all these things knocking around in my head right now. Do you have a place I could lie down? I don't feel well and I think maybe I need to rest."

How… Convenient. "I do. Let me show you to a room." I lead her upstairs and to a room at the far end of the west wing.

"Where is your room? Are you near? Will I see you when I wake up?" Pru asks, standing in the hall and eyeing the doorknob as though worried I will lock her in once she walks in.

"My room is in another part of the house. I live here. You will see me, I am sure. Dinner is served at 10. If you set an alarm to wake you, then you may join us. However, Fate will be there as well. Whatever is between the two of you is not to be fought over in my home. If you can not be civil toward her, then I will have your dinner sent to you."

"Don't you worry, son. I will be the best mom ever! You won't have to worry about me embarrassing you at the dinner table. I will wear my very best manners out to have our first dinner together." She grabs me in a hug and just as quickly releases me, stepping into her room and closing the door behind her.

I head directly for Fate's room. I knock gently on her

door; she answers quickly. I can't help myself and reach out to stroke her beautiful face. My hand encounters a barrier before it goes over the threshold. My face must have shown my surprise because Fate says, "I have shielded my room to keep Pru out. Has she gone?"

"So that is the ability you were gifted with? You can create shields. Fascinating. No, Pru is not gone. She is in a room at the far end of the west wing. She had the memories from her past lives restored and they are still knocking around in her head. She said she needs to rest. I don't think she has any intention of leaving any time soon. I told her that dinner would be at ten, but she had to be on her best behavior. It was… creepy. The way she said she would behave, but an agreement is an agreement. I came to warn you that she would be here tonight."

"Hmm, well, thank you. I think I will be shielded at dinner too. How did she react when you told her I am here?"

"Explosively. It was interesting, to say the least. I am glad we were able to have our first evening together alone, I am sorry it wasn't more romantic."

She shakes her head at me, "Charles, while it is true that I came willingly with you, it was still against my will. You threatened the lives of my people to persuade me to come here. Most people call that blackmail or coercion. Often it is called kidnapping. I am not being mean to you because I don't see how it would accomplish anything. A romantic dinner is not going to change that."

"I understand. I hope one day you will change your mind."

"Holding me hostage in a gilded cage is not the way to make that happen, Charles." She steps back and shuts the door in my face. Rude behavior when I have been so kind to her. I suppose I can't blame her, I am holding her prisoner here. I would not be as polite as she has been so far. Chances are I would be clawing my way out of here.

Four

Memré

My eyes hurt from all the time spent sitting here in front of
this computer. But I am going to find this guy that took
Fate and he is going to pay. Over and over again until we
have her back. I need food. Starting another search, I step
away from the computer and head for the kitchen. Thank-
fully, I keep only healthy foods in here, because there is no
way I would be able to resist the siren call of the junk food
right now. Opening the fridge, I see that I have been holed
up in here for way too long. I have a few carrots left and
some mushrooms. I pull those out along with the ranch and
set them on the counter near the cutting board. Checking
the pantry, I find some crunchy puffed peas. Those will be
great with the ranch. A few minutes later I have chopped

the veggies and plated them along with the peas. Pouring some ranch into a small dish I deem my meal complete. Food of champions.

Sitting down in front of the computer again, I see the search is done. I pull up the results and boom. There he is. I've got you now, Charles! Now that I have him identified I can track his sticky little fingers through everything he has going on and it takes very little time once I have identified him. Oh Charles, what kind of things are you doing? Those deposits don't appear to have a reason. I wonder if he has been paying taxes? We'll save that for another round. Right now, I just want to find all his money. Hope he has a stash of cash because I am about to shut his money down.

Cracking my knuckles I get to work, as his accounts pop up I hack the log-ins and start the process of cutting off his access. He will be able to fix it, but it will be a lot of hassle and he will have to go tend to it in person. He will have a severe cash shortage very soon though. I think I will get his utilities shut off too. This is going to be so much fun! I never get to fuck with the bad guys like this! He isn't going to know what hit him.

I should probably let people know where his houses are, I will get to that when I get finished here.

Fate

Sitting in my room, knowing Pru is in the same house I am being held prisoner in is weird. Especially since obviously she must know by now that I am being held prisoner by Charles. She was only mad that I was here. Super-duper sister behavior there. I can't believe this. I need my people. Walking over to the drawer with my phone in it, I open it and release the surrounding shield. Grabbing it, I turn it on as I pop a second shield into existence, this one just around me to keep my conversation private. The phone is finally booted up. Unlocking it with my face I tap the screen a few times and call Devon. I just need to hear his voice.

"Fate! Fate! Is that you? Fate, baby, are you ok?"

"Oh Devon, I just needed to hear your voice. Yes, I am fine. As well as I can be, considering. Things are weird here. And they just get more strange by the minute. Pru is here."

"What? He kidnapped your sister too? Why?"

"No, he didn't kidnap her. She showed up today. Apparently she went to a witch after she left us and got all of her prior memories unlocked. So she has all that mess knocking around in there, but that isn't the half of it. She claims that she is Charles' *mother*."

"No way. Charles' mother reincarnated as your sister? Are you kidding me? This is not the time to joke Fate, and this one is not a good one."

"Yeah, well, the joke is on me. She is settling right on in. Charles gave her a room as far away from mine as possible, but I am keeping my room shielded anyway. And myself when I leave my room."

"You aren't joking then? Wow. Gretchen is there, wrapped up in Pru. This is so bizarre. What could it mean, that everyone is being thrown together like this?"

"It gets weirder. He told me that Pru was here, but I had already heard her screeching when his father showed up and she lost her damn mind over him being here. Apparently this is the first time he has darkened Charles' door in a very long time. Any strangeness been happening at home?"

"I love it that you consider this home. I love hearing you. I wish you could come home. No, nothing strange."

"I have an idea of where I am. But I really think I can talk Charles around and that would be the best for all of us, if we could make Charles an ally instead of an enemy."

Five

FATE

Devon is silent for a moment, "I suppose it would, but I don't know how I will be able to trust him."

I feel something slam into my room shield just then, "Devon, I have to go. Something just slammed into my shield. I don't have any idea what it was, but I need to check it out."

"What? Fate, be careful. I love you!"

"I love you too." I hang up the phone, and I can hear Pru outside my door screeching. I hit the button to turn it off and then put my phone away, throwing another shield around it. Slamming the drawer shut, I walk over to the door, trying to compose myself as best I can before I open it.

Opening the door, I see Pru screeching and throwing herself at the door; I am so thankful for my shields. I feel Charles and some of his guard running this way, so I just lean against the wall and watch.

I see Charles and company clearing the top of the stairs and stopping to watch, their jaws dropped and eyes wide at the spectacle of Pru throwing herself at the shield while screeching "What are you hiding Fate? Let me in, Fate! It is my job to monitor you! You must submit!"

Charles is the first to recover, and he says something to his men. Two of them hand their guns to the others and come over to grab Pru. Each one taking an arm and marching her down the stairs. Charles walks over to my doorway, "What happened?"

"I don't know exactly. I was in here and I felt something hit my shield. By the time I got to my door…" I shrug and gesture in the direction they took Pru off in.

"I see. What was that she was screaming about? Has she always had lungs like that?"

"She was saying she wants to pry my head open and have a look at my thoughts. As for her lungs, yes. They have always been strong."

"One last question. Was she always like this or is it new?"

"I am not sure. But I think you have your mother to tend to so I will bid you good day, sir."

Charles

Fate just shut her door in my face. I want to be mad at her, but I really don't have the time. I can hear Pru getting wound up down there. What if she really is my mother, reincarnated? How in the nine planets did she and my father manage to show up separately on the exact same day? She recognized him immediately. That ticks a checkbox in the really is my mother column. The only other person alive that has ever seen both my mother and my father is Devon. I feel certain that if he knew where I am holding Fate, he wouldn't send an obviously mentally unstable woman in his place.

At the door to the sitting room Pru is pitching a fit in, I stop and just stare. She is stomping back and forth in the room, waving her hands while shouting that she has a right to see her son and her sister. Boy, that makes everything I want to do with Fate sound like incest. Ew. That reminds me, I need to ask Fate about why her looks suddenly changed so drastically. I'm not mad. She is hotter than she was during the time when she was pale and average. I step into the sitting room and clear my throat. Pru notices me and immediately sits down, placing her hands in her lap. I don't understand the effect I seem to have on her, but we are going to have to find a way for her to contain herself without my presence.

Sitting down across from her, I say, "Pru. You can't act like this. Period. I don't know or care why you and Fate fell out but you are going to need to control yourself. My house is not your battleground. I know you say you are my mother, reincarnated, but I have my doubts. What proof do you have? You say you have all these memories knocking around in your head, tell me about when I was a child. Tell me about the day you died. Help me to believe you because I am really wondering if you aren't just a plant."

"Oh, my sweet Charles. You wound your mother to the quick. If it is a story you want, it is a story you will get. You always did love my stories. The day I passed from my life as your birth mother, we had gone to the market square. I didn't want to because I knew the debtors were after your father again. They had no qualms about hurting me to get to him, only it didn't really get to him. He was never concerned about my health or yours. We only had money for food because I was taking in laundry. I took you boys because sometimes having you with me would deter them, but that day they weren't looking to hound me or harass me. I saw him coming at me and I tried to get us lost in the crowd, but I wasn't fast enough. He ran up and did me with the knife, so quick. It almost didn't hurt. Then he was gone, and I was lying on the ground trying so hard to tell you to stay away from him. I don't know what I was thinking, it isn't like you had anywhere else to go."

I have settled back into my seat by the time she is done, my hands steepled in front of me, "Devon was there for that. You could have gotten that story from him. Tell me a story from a time that was only you and I. One that I would recall, not one from before I was aware."

"Such a suspicious boy. You were never so suspicious when you were little. What must life have done to you all these years to cause you to be so suspicious, and of your own mother." She sighs with an overdone lift and slump of her torso. "Ok, I have the story. When you were around six years old, you got into your father's tobacco. It was his pipe tobacco that, his special order fancy pipe tobacco. It did have a very nice smell to it. You spread it out on the floor to be grass for your army men. I near had an attack when I saw what you had done. Your father would have killed you and me both had he been the one to find it. So we picked it all up, and I put it in my strainer to get the dirt off it. We got it back in the tin and put it back just in time. Your father came walking in not two minutes later and immediately went to his pipe and tobacco because he said it had been a bull's ass of a day and why the hell didn't I have dinner ready."

I remember the day she speaks of; I remember how later in the evening he beat her because his dinner was late. I have never told that to anyone. I know she didn't get that story from Devon. Or anyone else. It was buried in the mists of time. Maybe she really is…

"I will admit to it being possible that you are my mother. That being the case, you may continue to stay here so that we may get to know one another. But you are going to have to behave. You can't go trying to attack people. Or I will throw you out. Possibly for good. Are we clear?"

"Yes, yes, my sweet boy. I will behave, and I will convince you that I am your mother. Did you know I haven't had another child in any other life that lived? I think it's because you were still in this body," she gestures at me, "and your soul wasn't free to be reborn. I was always meant to be your mother. Now, I assume the cook is preparing dinner since it will soon be time. I think I would like to go look over the preparations."

I nod, "You may, but you may not interfere or abuse my staff. Rico and Benny will accompany you for the rest of the night, in case you seem close to losing control."

Both of the men I assigned this task roll their eyes and then put on their best game faces, I have to work at not smirking. Pru says, "Oh, how wonderful to have these big vigorous men to show me around. You must take me on a tour of the grounds. They looked lovely, what little I saw as I arrived."

Six

Charles

I arrive at the O'Kierks bar and grill just in time for our meeting. I am not looking forward to this for so many reasons. I feel certain it is likely to be a good thing to get this all out in the open, still; I have a hard knot of dread sitting in my stomach. Stepping into the dimly lit interior, I feel him in the far corner immediately. A handy talent I was gifted with, I can feel all those in the magical community wherever they are, even when they try to hide themselves. The ones I am tied to, for whatever reason, I can find over much longer distances. My father isn't aware of that, and I prefer he never find out. I knew he was in town, and I didn't care. The only reason I didn't realize that he was at my door is because I was dealing with Pru at that moment.

I slide into the booth seat across from my father, "Hello Judson."

"Son." He tips his head at me, "It looks like you've done real well for yourself."

"I haven't done terribly. Is that why you searched me out? Do you need money?"

"No, I gave up gambling years ago. A hundred and fifty years ago, to be more exact. No, I came to tell you the truth and to make what amends I can. I wasn't a good person as a human, or even as a vampire for a long time. I think about the only good things I did then were creating you and then turning you. You seem to have turned out pretty well for all that you didn't get any kind of good start. I thought that if I turned you, at least you would have time. I honestly figured that leaving after I turned you was the best I could do by you."

"Perhaps. Who turned you? How did you come into this gift?"

"I don't know. I feel certain that they didn't intend to turn me. I was attacked one night, but I was used to being attacked and I fought like the devil himself. They put an arm around my head to stop me fighting while they drank their fill. But I bit the arm in front of me, I wasn't trying to drink it but plenty of their blood went down my throat anyway when the bite kicked in. They left me for dead in the alley, but I didn't die. I woke up the next morning wondering how the hell I was alive and how I didn't have my entire throat ripped out."

"I see. Why did you turn me?"

"I was feeling guilty for so many things. It was my

fault your mother died, and I knew it. But I let you blame your friend all the same."

"Wait, what? I just talked to Pru, she never said specifically that it was your fault."

"Well, not to speak ill of your mother, but she doesn't seem like she is doing all that well. It looks like the lights are on but the bats are still flying around in the house if you get my drift."

I nod, signaling the server, "I do. And you aren't wrong. She is about five gallons of crazy in a one gallon bucket right now. She got all her memories restored from all her lives and then became a vampire. I don't even know who the hell she convinced to turn her. But some asshole definitely did." The server stops a little away from the table, and I tell her we would both like whatever is good on tap and a sampler appetizer plate. She writes it down and assures us she will return shortly with our order. Looking back over at Judson, I say, "How was it your fault she died?"

"It was me they were after. I had run up some enormous debts with my gambling. I didn't know how I would ever get them paid, so I went into hiding. When they couldn't find me they went after her. Her death wiped my debts clean, but it dirtied my soul in a way I didn't expect. That's why I drank so much for so long. I wasn't able to cope."

"So it was you she was warning me against as she died —" The server drops our mugs and the appetizer platter on the table in front of us, asking if we need anything else.

"No, we are good, thanks." I watch her leave and turn back to Judson, "It was, wasn't it?"

"I am sure it was. We weren't allowed a divorce in those days, unless you had a lot of money. But even the ones with the money for it mostly just lived separate lives instead of facing the stigma of divorce. Or killed their spouse. That was a relatively acceptable way of getting a divorce too. I didn't see it as an option because I knew there was no way I could ever be as good for you as your mother was right then. She loved you something fierce."

"It would seem so. Pru told me today that in all the rest of her incarnations she has never had a child that lived. She believes it is because my soul wasn't available, that I was always meant to be her son. I don't know what to think about that. Especially as right now I am holding her sister hostage because I love her. It certainly complicates things and I don't need further complication as I took her from Devon, who is rightfully mad at me for all the times I murdered Fate in her past lives to take her from Devon for having been the reason why mother died."

"Oh son, Devon was a child like you. It was never his fault. Why are you holding that woman hostage? I don't think that is the way to her heart, son."

Taking a swig of my beer gives me time to think about my answer. But it isn't nearly enough time. Unable to stall further, I say, "It's complicated. Usually when Devon finds her, I just kill her and I am done with it. This time, this time, I couldn't. And I got to know her a little, a precious little. But that was enough to hook me, and I don't seem to be able to walk away from her or even kill her and be done with it. My house was peaceful until I brought her back, and even with all that noise and nonsense going on, I wouldn't trade her for anything."

My father peers at me like he can see past the physical and into my soul saying, "Son, nothing good comes from a person you can't put aside. Generally speaking, nothing good will have caused you to be unable to put a person aside. I only know of a few ways for this to happen- addiction, spells, or gods. Every damn one of them is trouble. Could it be one of those that has you wrapped around this woman?"

"No!" I look away from him, watching the few humans in here as they go about their business, "Maybe. I don't know. I don't know what it is that has me hooked on her, all I know is that I am. At this point, I don't even care if I have to share her. But I need to be in her light. When I talk to her… When I talk to her, it feels like the sun shining on me after decades of darkness. I… I can't let her go, and I don't even care what the reason is. I feel more clear now than I have in centuries. I don't know that I am ready to let go my grievance with Devon, because I might be shut out of her life if I do. It hasn't even been that long, but I don't know if I would survive it."

"That is not good. Not good at all, son. What are you going to do?"

I shrug, "Probably let her talk me into something stupid and try to stay in her life as best I can."

He tips his head to one side, "You talk and I think I

have it figured out, but then you blow that theory out of the water. I don't know what has you, but I hope you get it taken care of. I feel like it isn't my place to interfere in the ways that a father usually would because I haven't been much of a father. If you decide you would like aid, I am here and more than willing to be of assistance."

"I appreciate all of that, and I agree with the first part. But thank you."

"You're welcome, son. I think I will be going now, before anyone loses control and causes a scene. You have a good day and here is my card, call me if you need or want to talk to me."

Judson strides out the door before I can even ask what he meant about someone losing control, leaving me with his card, more questions, and the bill.

Seven

I SIGNAL the server for the check. She gives me a wave to let me know she has seen me. I take a swig of my beer while I wait and as I lower it Pru appears in front of me.

"Did you just blink your way in here? You know you can't do that, right? Please tell me you did not do that." I put an elbow on the table and forehead in that hand. What the hell am I going to do with this lady that says she is my mother?

"Of course I didn't blink in," she says as she takes the seat so recently vacated by my father, "I have been here the whole time. I wanted to watch over you while you met with him. He is a dirty bastard and I don't trust him. You shouldn't either."

"What? You were here spying on me? That is not cool. And it isn't something I am going to tolerate. Why would you think that kind of behavior is acceptable?" I suppose it does explain Judson's parting remark about someone losing control.

"Oh my sweet boy, I am just watching over you. Making sure you are safe, that's all. Besides, I wanted to make sure he told you the truth about his part in my death."

"So you were spying. Eavesdropping. Invading my privacy. Listen, I don't know what gave you the idea that it was acceptable to do this sort of thing, but this is the height of bad manners. What you are doing is wrong. W-R-O-N-G. Do you understand?"

She sighs like she is exasperated with me, "Charles, I am your mother. This is what moms do. This is what families do. Trust me. I have been part of a family a lot more than you have, families spy on each other. More even than what I have done today, it is what they do."

"What kind of family were you in? That is not what they do. Families treat each other with respect and courtesy. They love each other. They support each other. They lift up those that fall. Families do not spy on each other. If that is what your family did, family might be the wrong label." I rub the bridge of my nose, "New subject." The server shows up just then, I hand her my card, and she takes it away, "You told me that you got a witch to restore, no, unlock all your memories from past lives. Were you a vampire before that, or were you turned after?"

"Nosy today, aren't you? But I suppose I can tell you a little. I was turned after my memories were unlocked. Before I knew that you were here, I had no reason to want to stay here. I had no one. Tricksy Fate had her memories, but I didn't even have that. Now I have the memories and I have you, sweet boy." Pru leans across the table to pat my cheek. This is so weird. I don't like it when she touches me, so I take her hand and place it on the table. On her side of the table.

"I think I understand that now. But how did you know I was your son? You never saw me as an adult."

She waves a hand at me, "Pfft, that was easy. I had the witch scry for me. I asked her what happened to the only child I ever had that lived, and when she looked in the water, she saw you. After that, a simple location spell with some of my blood, because you are my child it doesn't matter if I have changed bodies a few times."

"How… interesting. How did you find a vampire to change you so quickly after that?"

She waggles a finger at me, "No, no, you're not getting all my secrets, mister. A vampire never tells who turned them."

My jaw drops, "What are you talking about?"

"My sire told me that I shouldn't share freely who turned me. That should be private. They said that turning connected the sire to their fledgling for a time and that would be a weakness. Possible leverage for the less princi-pled among us."

"Um, no. That isn't how it works. But keep your secrets, it makes no difference to me. Though I am glad that as your only child that lived I haven't been reborn and you suddenly wandered up talking about being my mother in another life. I can only imagine how that would have gone."

Pru's mouth turns down at the corners, "You act like you aren't happy to see me, son." Her voice has risen with each word, and the other customers have turned to look at us. The server takes this moment to bring back my card, nearly throwing it down on the table before running away.

"Pru, why don't I take you shopping? We could get you a whole new wardrobe to go with your whole new life?"

Still pouting, she crosses her arms and says, "Only if you say please mother."

What? Oh for fuck's sake. I know I have done some awful shit in my life, but damn, what did I do to deserve this? Oh yeah, I spent a lot of time hunting Fate down and killing her. Well then, fair enough, I suppose. Ugh, I still don't like this. "Please mother, let me take you shopping." The muscles in my jaw are ticking wildly as Pru pretends to think about it before extending her hand and waiting for me to help her out of the booth. Once she is up I hustle her out of the place, so if she is going to create a scene it will at least not be in such close quarters.

Eight

I stare at the phone like it will show me Fate after she hangs up so quickly. Is she okay? What hit her shields? I just need her back with me. Pushing away from my desk, I stand and walk out of my office, heading downstairs and toward the kitchen. Natasha and company don't stay in Fate's office now that she isn't here with them. I think they miss her too. I know they do. It is difficult for me to get past my own issues here. Hard for me to believe that she isn't dead again, only kidnapped… Though I don't know if that will be a better thing in the long run. What if his plan works? What if she falls in love with him? What will I do if she decides not to come back? I have to stop midway down the stairs, my thoughts hurting me so much it is like a physical pain. Deep breaths, one-two-three-four-five. Breathe slow, inhale slow and exhale slow. Getting myself together, I make it to the kitchen without further intrusive thoughts about the worst possible outcome. Natasha and Ajah are working at the island, still looking for the right locator spell I imagine. Ajah is no witch, but she is great at researching things, so she helps Natasha a lot these days. Chances are that when, yes, that's it, when Fate gets back, Ajah will retire from the bodyguard role and take an assistant role. I clear my throat as I walk in, to be sure they are aware that I am here and so that I do not intrude on any private conversations. The women look up at me and I say, "Fate called me."

Natasha straightens and gives me her full attention, as does Ajah, "So what did she say, man? Don't leave Ajah and I in the dark!"

"Well, things are really eventful over at Charles' place. She has a possible idea of where she is now, but she doesn't want us to come get her, she feels certain that she can convince Charles to bring her back."

I watch as Natasha and Ajah share a look, then Ajah says, "It is possible. He did all this to get to her. I know all the other times he was just trying to kill her to get back at you, but in this case you are not the primary target. He wanted Fate. He swore a blood oath so she would go with him. And he had us pretty screwed. His men could have killed you and Billy, and he literally had Natasha by the throat. Once she agreed to go with him, he was done. I wouldn't underestimate the power she has over him."

That's something my demons will be bringing up on a regular basis, I am sure. "I hope she can manage to get him to bring her back. In the meantime, I still want to work on plan A. How is that going?"

Natasha shrugs, "Like shit. Grams hasn't gotten back to me and I am not finding anything. This would be so much easier if we had someone handy that shared her bloodline. Since we don't, it is a royal pain in the ass."

"Damn. Well, she told me another interesting tidbit about the goings on over there. Pru showed up claiming to be Charles' long dead mother."

Natasha and Ajah's eyes go round like saucers, both exclaiming, "What?"

"Yeah, from what I gather when she left here, she went to another witch and had her memories from her past lives unlocked and then got herself turned into a vampire. Shortly after that, she found Charles and is claiming to be his mother. It has got to be the strangest thing I have ever heard, and I have heard some things."

"I… just… wow." Natasha shakes her head, "How did she decide he was her kid?"

"I have no idea. Fate had to get off the phone pretty quickly. She was in her room and had shielded it to ensure privacy, but something weird hit her shields. With Pru being there and still mad at Fate, I feel certain that it was probably her."

"Damn. That makes being there dangerous for Fate all over again. But if she is shielding her room, then maybe she is shielding herself when she is not in her room."

Natasha starts to pace, "We need to find her faster than this. I just don't know how! Dammit! Why couldn't it just be set this thing on fire and the smoke will lead you there? Nooooo, has to be all damn difficult, and the spells that would work the best require some part of Fate or a family member. Unfortunately, she had cleaned out her hairbrush the day she was kidnapped, so there is nothing there. The one fucking time she actually cleans out her hairbrush! I mean, it is a good sign, because she only stopped when Charlie died, before that she did it regularly. It's just so damn inconvenient right now!"

Ajah is the one that starts laughing. Natasha stops in her tracks when the laughter starts, glaring at Ajah. Ajah just laughs harder, "You're — hahahahaha — mad at her — gasp — hahaha — for cleaning — hahahaha — her hairbrush — hahahahahahah!"

By the time she gets out what is funny I am laughing and even Natasha is grinning, looking sheepish.

We manage to calm down and Natasha says, "I guess this is getting to me too. I miss my friend. We have been working together for so long, I feel like part of me is missing."

I nod, "I feel like part of me is missing too. It is awful and the only cure for it is for her to come back. One other thing, she said, that the more she sees of Pru, the more certain she is that she doesn't have a way to save Pru from herself."

Natasha's hand flies to cover her mouth, "Oh no, that is terrible. Fucking Charles! Fate needs us right now while she is dealing with this. I might let Grams curse his ass when we get Fate back."

A noise like a single firecracker exploding comes from one of the front rooms of the house, sending all the shifters running that way as they shift and the rest of us not far behind.

Later that day.

"Shit! Is that the time? Ajah, get a vehicle ready. We have to go meet with Maggie and we are definitely going to be late to the party. Ryna, you want to come along? Ajah, maybe we should take one of the guys to get them out of the house?" I say all this as I am slamming books and computers closed, gathering them all up and leaving the room. I have no idea what their answers were. Stepping into Fate's office I turn to the left and step through to the magic room. I set everything down on the desk in there before I run down the hall to Devon's office. Popping my head in I say, "Billy, could you come downstairs for a moment?" Then I head downstairs without waiting to see if he follows. If he does, then he will know where I have gone, if not I will talk to him when I get back. I stop at the front door, Billy is no more than a second or two behind me.

"What's up, Tash?"

"Ugh. I do not like that nickname. Keep trying. I have to go look at the thing with Maggie. Remember?"

He looks puzzled for a second then, "Oooh! Yes. Wonderful. Take lots of pictures, tell the ghost lady that I said hello. I will keep Devon upstairs and distracted. We are going through all his financial holdings. They are extensive, but poorly managed. It will be a week or three with the way he is distracted." He pulls me into his arms, pressing his lips against mine. The sweet, small goodbye kiss is not enough and only sparks a flame in the two of us. Our lips tease and play, nibbles of delight and promise before I put my hands agains his chest and push him away. Breathing heavier I say, "Going to have to take a rain check on that, I really am late."

He smiles that wide smile of his and my core clenches as he says, "I'll be waiting for you with bells on."

I groan as I open the door and step out into the bright sunlight. Leaning back in the door I grab my purse and sunglasses from the table and shut the door behind me as I dash over to the Suburban. As soon as my door is closed Ajah backs down the drive. I smile to see Ryna sitting up front with her. Owen is in the backseat across from me. I pull up the address Maggie sent me and pass my phone up to Ryna. She enters it into the gps as we head in the general direction of the major highways before passing my phone back to me. Ajah gets us heading in the right direction and I send a text to Maggie, telling her that I am running late but on the way. I get a text back before I can drop it back in my purse. It is a laugh emoji. Of course. A second text comes in that says she figured it was possible we would be late because it is still a secret from Devon.

Ten minutes later we pull up to a gated drive, the gate opens as we get to the security box so Ajah drives us through. As we round a bend in the drive the main house comes into view. It is huge. A more greek revival style house, with clean lines and gorgeous detail work. Ajah comes to a smooth stop behind Maggie's car. Getting out we walk over to the porch where Maggie waits.

"Hi," she says as she hugs each of us in greeting, "I have opened the house already. The lady is inside waiting to interview you, Natasha. She says too many people at once is draining and she has trouble focusing. So she would like for you to go in and have a chat with her. If you two come to an agreement, then she will hang back a watch without interacting this time so as to conserve her energy. Sound good?"

"Yeah, I like it. Hopefully," I say as I open the door, "I will be out shortly with good news." Stepping over the threshold I close the door behind me. "Hello? Maggie didn't mention your name, I am Natasha." The woman appears in front of me, a few feet further into the house. "Oh, there you are. I would offer to shake your hand but I don't know how well that will work. May I ask your name?"

Her voice is soft and low, I don't know if I would have heard her if I wasn't a vampire. She says, "My name is Penelope. What will you do with this place if you and your mistress buy it?" Her style of dress is old enough that I think she has been here haunting a very long time.

"We plan to make it a home. Every one of us that

would live here is part of the magical community in some way. We don't have any children or pets, though I can't promise they won't ever happen. Well, we do have the shifters, but I don't know that they count as pets."

She chuckles at my joke, "You won't tear it down or turn it into a museum with crowds tromping through?"

"No. It will be plenty busy, but mostly with the same people. We are a large group. And, we would have no choice but to make repairs. The current owners have not been caring for your home."

I see the flash of anger on her face, "I know! They left it to ruin and only came here for political parties. They were disgusting! I won't repeat what they did, but I made them all sorry they were here. I find you and your family acceptable. I grant permission and I won't scare away the workers who come to repair the place." She places a hand on a banister, "It will be good to see it renewed. I must go now. Staying visible for this long after being alone for so long is tiring. Thank you, I look forward to hearing the sounds of family again."

The lady fades away. She seems so sweet, but so angry about those parties. I can't help but wonder what they were doing. I turn back to the door after saying "Thank you" into the air, hoping she heard even if she doesn't respond. Opening the door I invite everyone in saying, "She likes us. Let's check out the house. I think it will be perfect, but I want to show her pictures when she gets back. And Billy too, he wants to see pictures. I can't wait to see Devon's face when she surprises him with this." Everyone files in and we take stock. The ceilings are soaring, gorgeous chandeliers in desperate need of cleaning are everywhere. We wander through the downstairs, our steps echo through the rooms. The place is mostly unfurnished. The kitchen is enormous. Maria will be extra pleased. Maggie tells me that there are multiple small homes on the property. They were for hired help, one of the things she found to be a selling point is that this place never held slaves for labor. They did however, hide some. There are passages from the basement and various other parts of the house that lead to the other homes and a couple that come out in specific parts of the property.

We see multiple sitting rooms and a ballroom, as well as a glorious library. Heading upstairs the bedrooms are everywhere, as are the bathrooms. This place is huge. Maggie tells us that Penelope told her there are secret passages in most of the rooms and that there are a couple of rooms that are only accessible by secret passage. The huge clawfoot bathtubs in the majority of the bathrooms would have sold me. But this place is fucking awesome.

As we head back to the front door I tell Maggie, "Send the offer. For the listing price or whatever you think is best. I want to get this place bought now and have the workers start on it immediately. I am authorized to act for Fate in this, have your uncle draw up the contracts and let's get it done. Then you get people out here to inspect every inch of this place and then to restore it. Fate will want this to remain as original as possible without sacrificing the integrity of the house." I stop before stepping out the front door, "Thank you Penelope, we look forward to seeing you again soon." I could swear I hear a sigh of contentment as I step through the door and Maggie closes it behind us. She is pulling out her phone and calling the other agent, waving bye to us as she sets to work on getting Fate the best deal possible.

I take one more long look at the house, my heart swells with joy knowing this will be waiting for Fate when she comes back home.

Nine

I finally make it into the room where the noise came from
to see someone standing in the middle of the couch
wreathed by smoke, coughing and trying to bat it away.
Steve, John, Owen, and Brad have surrounded the person
on the couch while Ajah and Ryna are standing next to
each other, both poised to strike. The two of them, golden,
tiny, fierce lady and giant tiger standing side by side; they
look more dangerous than the rest of the room. The smoke
finally clears around the sputtering person and reveals
them to be… Grams?

"Grams! What are you doing popping in like this?" I
realize what is about to happen but there is nothing that
will stop what Grams is about to say. I try anyway, "Guys,

it's my Grams. Shift back, for the love of Goddess, shift back now!"

"Puppies!" Grams gets a look around and seeing all the shifters is delighted to find puppies. "And a bear! And tigers! I feel like Dorothy, can I pet them?"

I hurry over to help Grams down from the couch before she breaks a hip falling or gets bit by a shifter for trying to pet them. For their part, all the shifters back up a bit, out of the range of Grams questing hands. Except for Owen, who carefully steps around furniture to come close enough for Grams to reach him. She is delighted and buries her hands in his fur, giving him a good scratch and making sure to get behind his ears. She hugs him and plants a kiss on the top of his head, "I never knew a shifter that didn't love a good scratch once they allowed it. You are sweet boy and a credit to your family." She gives him one more scratch on his head and turns to me, "I think I found something."

"That's wonderful! Why didn't you drive over? Or call? I would come get you."

Grams looks away, like she doesn't want me to see her eyes and says, "I might have gotten my license taken away after I hit that bitch Fannie Mae. I didn't want anyone to know, so I kept it quiet. The cops think I did it by accident, because I'm old and senile. But me and Fannie Mae know the truth. She screeched like a harpy when she heard me pretending it was an accident." She looks back at me and shrugs, "They took my license so now I don't drive."

I want to be mad at her, I really do. She could have

been hurt. Fannie Mae, well, that bitch is solid and I am guessing she didn't die. "Grams. What did Fannie Mae do this time?"

"She said bad things about your mother's lack of magic use and the cast aspersions' on your parentage. She should be glad I only hit her once."

"Damn Grams, you fierce." Owen gives her a thumbs up, and she returns the gesture, grinning like the madwoman she is.

She reaches over and pats his cheek, "Such a good boy you are. I bet your mom is so proud."

I hear Brad mumble "Kiss-ass."

I think now might be a great time to get Grams to the kitchen. "Come on Grams, let's get you some tea. In the kitchen. Away from all the shifters." I half drag her out of the room and down the hall to the kitchen.

Ten

Ryna and Ajah have come to the kitchen to hear what Grams has to say, but everyone else has drifted back off to whatever else they have going on. After getting her seated, I work on making Grams a hot cup of tea, the good green from Stash. It is her favorite kind, and I have enough memories associated with it I keep it in the house for my own consumption. Tea made for everyone, I place all the cups on a tray and bring them to the island. Passing out the teas, I ask Grams, "So, what did you find?"

"I found a spell that I think might do the trick. After you left I got to thinking about the books I have at the house. I have been through most of them at some point, because I like to learn new things. It took me some time to find the right book and the spell within the book, but I think this will work. It needs to be done in a during the new moon and the more contact the witches that cast the spell had with her before she disappeared, the better."

"Memré and Maggie along with you should work, right Natasha?"

Jumping at the sound of a male voice, I see Devon standing in the doorway, "Sure would be great if you could make some noise walking through the house, Devon. Yes, Maggie and Memré would work great."

He walks in and sits on one of the stools around the island, "Do you think this will find her?"

Griselda looks at Devon, "Yes, dear boy, I do. Goodness, you do resemble my Fernando. Maybe you were related somewhere along the line. How are you holding up?"

I can feel my eyes rounding with horror as she tells Devon that he looks similar to Grandpa Fernando. Please Grams, for the love of all that's holy, please do not hit on him.

Devon smiles a little at my facial expression before he replies, "I miss her. It is a hole ripped back open, and it was only just healing. At this point I am somewhat cracked around the edges, but I am holding together."

"It will all resolve itself, don't you worry. Now," Griselda puts her hands out in front of her over the island and a book pops into them from elsewhere, "Here is the book. I know you will add it to the collection, as it should be. Now, I am tired. Who is going to drive me home? I don't think I have another poof in me."

Ajah chimes in, "I can give you a ride home. Come on outside when you are ready, I'll get the suburban out."

Ryna stops her, "Mind if I ride with you?"

Ajah's whole face lights up, "Um. no. I mean. Sure. Yes. You are welcome to ride with me."

Ryna smiles widely at Ajah and the two walk out together. I look over to Grams and Devon, "Well. That was interesting. Should be a fun ride home Grams."

She laughs, "All the sex in the air should at least keep me awake until I get home."

Ajah

"Here you go Grams, I worried that the suburban might be a little too tall for you to get in easily, I brought a step stool." I found a two-step stool made of plastic in the garage. As soon as I saw it I knew Grams would need it, especially since Ryna was eyeing it. She is so tiny, I feel like a frigging giant next to her. Even if I am only a few inches taller than her. She is gorgeous, with that golden coloring of hers. I always thought that golden as a color description for people was garbage in all the books I read, now I think maybe they saw Ryna. Her long hair flows down her back, looking like spun gold. Her skin has this golden hue to it I have never seen on another person. And yet, for as tiny and golden as she is, she dressed in all black. Figure hugging sheath and stilettos to match. I think I'm in lust.

Griselda makes it into the truck and I scoop up the stool, closing her door I walk to the back of the truck and stow it in the hatch. For all that Ryna was eyeing the stool, she hopped right up into the back seat and it took me a minute to remember how to breathe after seeing her butt in the air as she got in. Shaking my head to clear it, I make it to the driver's side and get in. The trip over to Griselda's is largely uneventful. We talk, she asks about my family and offers her condolences upon finding out they are dead. She is a sweet lady; I see why Natasha adores her. Pulling into the drive, I put the truck in park but leave it running as I grab the stool from the back and assist Griselda in getting out of the truck. All I really did was provide a hand for balance, but she seemed appreciative. Walking her to the door, she tells me, "You two are adorable. You know she likes you?"

"Wha-at exactly do you mean Griselda?"

She stops in front of her door, waves it open and says, "I mean, that girl likes you as much as you like her. It is as plain as the nose on my face. Now go woo her." She gives me a pat on my shoulder and walks into her house muttering, "Children. I need a nap."

I realize I have been staring at Griselda's closed door for much longer than I could do with no one noticing, and better yet, my jaw is hanging open. I rub the bridge of my nose and head for the truck.

As I get in Ryna says, "What did she hit you with? I love older people. They are aware that their time grows short and they become so much more outspoken. It is really fun when they were outspoken to begin with. So what did she say?"

I feel the heat in my cheeks; they are on fire. Might as well rip off the band-aid. "She said that you like me as much as I like you, and I should do something about that. Oh, and that we are adorable."

I peek over at Ryna, the silence scares me. She is still looking at me, only with her jaw hanging open and her eyes wide open as they get. I reach over and gently push her chin up with one finger and then place my hand back on the steering wheel as I try to remember not to grip it so tightly I crush the thing. Oh Goddess, what if I fucked up saying that?

"How did she know?"

"Um, she's a witch? How do they know anything? I don't know. Honestly still a little freaked out over what Pru was trying to do to people with her mind reading."

"With her what?"

"Pru was a mind reader. Except she was using her abilities to do bad things."

"Was. You said was. Did something happen to her powers?"

"Yeah... They took them away. I was there when it all

happened. Pru was trying to bash her way into people's minds and had been bashing her way into Fate's mind for a long time. Griselda was actually the one that passed the spell to take away her abilities to Fate. Fate wanted nothing to do with it until she found out that Pru had been in on all the things Charlie, her now dead husband, had been doing. Though really, she probably wouldn't have done it even then if Pru hadn't come by and lost her shit when she figured out she couldn't read everyone's mind anymore."

"That is a lot. Did Fate not know that Pru was doing wrong?"

"It wasn't so much a matter of knowing as it was that she thought it was just her that Pru did it to, a sister thing. Even that had become too much for her, and that was why she talked to Griselda. She wanted a spell to keep her sister out of her mind. Griselda gave her that spell and the one to take away her powers. It was a pretty vicious spell, and they said that the warning for using it was that if you were using it for poor reasons, it would rebound and take your powers away."

"I can see how that would be a deterrent to using it for jealousy or some other specious reason. As for what Griselda said to you, well, I am interested in you."

"You are? I mean, you are. Where do you want to go with that?"

"I think I would like to go slow. Things are a bit strange right now. I am not sure of getting close to anyone, really. There are some things I do that others… may find odd. Or distasteful. Definitely illegal. I have no intentions of stopping those things but, it will take a good deal of trust before I am willing to share that. How about we get to know each other for a while and during that time, you decide where you would draw the line?"

"I feel pretty certain on where I draw the line, but sure. It's as good a plan as any. I have never seen a plan work all that great where love is concerned, but let's give it a shot." I chuckle at the thought of trying to plan out a relationship as I pull the suburban into the garage. Hopping out, I realize I forgot the damn stool in Griselda's driveway. "Damn it. Tell everyone—" I cut off telling Ryna that I was going back to Griselda's when she comes around the truck carrying the stool.

She holds it out to me, "I picked it up and set it in the back seat after I crawled through to the front seat."

"Thank you so much. I did not want to go all the way back over there for a stool in the driveway."

Seamus is in the doorway watching us as we walk up, he is grinning but Ryna growls at him. She says, "Can you not find a pair of pants made in this decade?"

His grin stretches impossibly wider, "They all seem to be hiding from me, haven't been able to spot one in the wild."

I can't help but laugh and Ryna narrows her eyes at me, telling him, "Your dick is hanging out."

He jumps to cover himself and I laugh harder, knowing that she just lied to him. He hustles off into the interior of the house and I ask her, "Why did he just believe you? He didn't even check?"

Now she laughs, "He believed me because the last time he didn't I made it true."

I tip my head to one side, "Did you snatch the pants off him?"

"No. I cut them from groin to ankle."

"But you don't have a knife on you right now."

"Says who?"

"It doesn't look like you have one hidden anywhere."

"Looks are deceiving and I can assure you, I *always* have a knife."

"Goddess, that is sexy." She walks off with a smug smile as I close the front door. What a woman.

Eleven

I can feel Charles heading this way, so I open a space in front of the library door so he may enter unimpeded without even looking up from my book. I am reading a fascinating book called Ovid Metamorphoses. It is inspiring, and I wonder if the author was a part of the magical community. Charles makes it in the room and I close the hole, can't have my darling sister in here trying to kill me again.

Stopping a couple feet from me he asks, "That shield thing you do, how does it work?"

Taking my eyes from the book I look up at him, he really is handsome in the Apollo sort of way. He seems very concerned right now so I bite back the sarcasm that is always ready to fly free these past few days, "I couldn't guess at the dynamics of it. Is there a specific thing you want to know, Charles?"

"Well, I want to have a conversation with you that cannot be eavesdropped upon and I don't want anyone to wander in looking for me. I am unsure as to whether you can maintain the shield over your bedroom while shielding this room as well?"

"Yes, I can do that. Would you like me to shield the room?"

His shoulder slump as he exhales, "Yes, please."

His relief is a bit concerning, so I wave my hand as though I am setting the shield that is already in place and he walks over to the liquor cabinet, helping himself to a half full rocks glass of that good Scottish Balvenie whiskey he keeps in here. He turns and holds up the bottle at me, raising his brows to ask if I would like a drink. I tell him I would and he pours another rocks glass, but less full than his.

He brings my glass over and sets it on the table next to me before retreating to the chair across from me, the one that is overlarge and facing the windows. He sinks down into the chair and takes a fairly large swig from his cup. He must be distressed to drink it that way. He is silent and staring out the window while he drinks, so I take a sip of my own and go back to Ovid.

A few stories later he says, "Pru has taken to following me everywhere. I went to meet with my father and she was there too. She revealed herself after she listened to the entire conversation we had."

"Oh my. That is rather like her, though. Her parents were not kind to her."

He looks at me with his face crinkled up, "Why do you say her parents?"

"Because they are her parents and not mine."

"I didn't see anything about that in the file I got from the investigator."

"Well, that is because my parents adopted me in Armenia and when they came back stateside they just bought an Armenian birth certificate before they left."

"I have another question about you, that is rather personal. I hope you will forgive me but, why did your coloring change so drastically and why don't you need glasses anymore?"

"Ah, that is a whole thing. I don't care about the question. It is a rather drastic change. Apparently, my parents were not the happiest about my coloring and they felt that I should look more like them. So they glamoured me. Like so strong a glamour that it affected my ability to see. As it weakened, I was losing my glasses all the time and as it turns out that was because my vision wasn't being interfered with by the glamour. When Griselda took the glamour off, well, poof. This is what I look like under all those layers of white."

"Why would your parents — I mean they, why would they do that?"

"Oh, who knows? I have lots of theories, but on the

scale of things, that wasn't really the worst thing they ever did."

"What?"

"Listen, I am only going to tell this story once and I don't know how many questions I will be willing to answer." I go on to tell him about my parents conceiving Pru and deciding I was evil. How they tried to bind me and were unsuccessful. How they set Pru to monitor me after her powers came in and how that eventually led to us taking away her powers. Charles face grows more serious as I go through the story, but he is quiet and does not interrupt. When I finish he is silent for a moment, as though digesting all that I have divulged.

"Taking away her powers, that is the falling out you had?"

I nod and sip my drink.

"My father told me it wasn't Devon's fault."

I almost drop my glass, but Balvenie is not to be wasted like that. I set it gently down and ask him to please explain.

He says, "All this time I thought Devon caused my mother's death. That is why I killed you so many times to get back at him. I don't know what to do now. How do I reconcile this information?"

"I don't have any good answers for you, Charles. I can see how that would throw anyone with your background for a loop."

"Yes. A loop. Thank you for listening. I know you are

still upset with the situation as it is but, I am not ready or able to let you go."

"I don't understand that, Charles. Not completely. I do feel some of the pull to keep you around, but that is dependent on you and Devon. I will leave you to think. The shield will stay in place until you place your hand on it, so you will be undisturbed."

"Thank you Fate, I don't deserve your kindness, but I appreciate it."

Shielding myself as I step out of the library, I wonder, will this be the catalyst to get me home? Considering how wrecked he is with this, can we leave him without anyone while dealing with my sister, his mother? I need to call Devon.

Twelve

FATE

Safe in my room, I put up the second barrier. I don't want anything to do with Pru listening at the door and since we took her powers; I feel like that is an eventuality since I am keeping a shield up and denying her access to my spaces. Phone out of the drawer I wait the eternity it takes for it to power up. Seconds later it is unlocked and I am pulling up Devon's number. He answers before the first ring finishes, "Fate! I miss you so much. Are you ok?"

"I am so much better hearing your voice. You soothe my soul."

"I love you. Can we come get you yet? Or have you talked him into bringing you home?"

"I love you too. No, don't come get me. I think He is

coming around." I spend the next few minutes telling Devon about my conversation with Charles, even the parts he might not like so much. He is silent while I speak, and for long moments after I've finished.

I hear him draw a deep breath and release it as he says, "What do you mean, you feel a pull?"

"I don't know how to describe it exactly beyond I feel like he is meant to stay with us. It isn't like with you, the ache from being away from you is deep and I feel that keenly all the time. With Charles it is more like there is a thread of fate pinging when I decide to leave him here without us."

"I can't say I like that idea, but if having him on our team and in our home will keep you alive, so be it. Just come home soon. Bring the jerk, but come home. Maybe I should give Natasha and company a warning that this might happen?"

"Hmm, I actually plan to call them after we finish talking. I haven't spoken to Natasha and Memré since I was taken, I need to talk to them too. Make sure our foundation creation is going as smoothly as it can." And check on that bigger house I asked Maggie to find for me.

"They will probably take it better from you than they would from me, anyway."

"I think they might. I should go, I can't stay on here too long, in case Pru comes looking for me."

"I love you, Fate. Come home."

"I love you so much. Soon."

Ending the call, I hold the phone to me for the feeling

of still being that much closer to him. I need to call Natasha and Memré, we all need to talk.

I call Natasha first, she answers quickly, "Are you ready for us to come get you yet?"

I laugh, "Not just yet. I think I am getting closer to him bringing me home. But that isn't what I called about."

"How and what did you call about then?"

"Let's get Memré in here too, so we can all discuss this stuff." Natasha handles getting Memré added to the call.

Memré starts off with, "Well Fate, I know where all his houses are. I think we could find you pretty quickly."

Gasping I say, "Oh no, you didn't?"

Natasha laughs, "You know she did Fate. She started working on it as soon as you were taken. I think she is slipping, it took her a minute."

"Of course I did! What else would I do?" I can almost see Memré shaking her head at me, "I will be the only one with access to his money by the end of the day, though that does not count any cash he has lying around. He should be glad that is all I have done so far."

I nod, "You're right. But, I need you to hold off on taking it all and let's see if I can get this resolved. Which is kind of what I called about. I think I can get him to bring me home on his own, but there is a catch."

Matching groans and Natasha says, "Of course there is a catch. What is the catch?"

"It feels like I have to keep him around? I don't understand it, but it feels like he has to be part of our lives too."

Memré snorts in disgust, "He is a drug dealer and a

kidnapper. He has an unhealthy fixation on you, whether it results in killing or kidnapping, it ain't healthy. Are you getting Stockholm's syndrome here?"

"No, I am not," I reply, my voice dry like my humor is right now, "It isn't like that. It feels like something is tying us together, and though it isn't sexual, it seems like it could go there fast. That is the part I wanted to talk to you two about. I have been mostly honest with Devon, though I did not tell him I felt like it could get sexual quickly. I didn't want him to be hurt or to worry. I am coming back to him and I won't do anything behind his back. But this, I don't know what to do with this? Help?"

Memré chuckles, "Natasha, I think this one might be on you. Of all of us, you have the most threesome experience."

"You can't see it, Memré, but you are getting the eye. Your pants would be on fire if you were here."

"Ha! Jokes on you! I'm not wearing any!"

Natasha groans and the laughter pours out of me, until it isn't laughter anymore and I am sobbing into my phone about how much I miss my family. Natasha and Memré make sympathetic noises till I get it all out of my system. Sniffling I say, "I don't know how much more I can take. This is all just so much and before I even get to process one thing, another happens. I miss all of you so much and Pru is here. She keeps having screaming outbursts and I hate her a little, I mean fuck, I can't even be kidnapped without her showing up to interfere." Realizing what I just said makes me chuckle. They are silent, probably waiting to see if I am going to lose it again. "Guys, it's ok, that last part was kind of funny. I think I have all the tears out now, I needed to talk to my friends. I really do miss you both so much."

"We miss you too. Did I mention that I know where all his houses are and we could show up there?" Memré laughs, "Even if it took a minute to figure out which one was the house he is keeping you in. Want to give us any clues? Is there a fence? A wall? Help a girl out!"

Natasha and I laugh and I tell them, "Yes, there is a wall. But no, don't come here. I think I am done feeling sorry for myself. I am just out of sorts with all the things. Give me a little longer and if I don't get him to bring me home, then you can come get me. But don't bring Devon, I feel like they will fight if Charles doesn't bring me home and I couldn't interfere, but I would hate to see it."

Natasha says, "I guess that is somewhat reasonable, considering the rest of this conversation. I want it noted that I don't like any of this. I think we should come and get you now and let Charles sort himself out on his own."

Memré added her two cents, "I agree. And I think having to dig himself out from twenty feet in the ground would be a real learning experience."

Thirteen

Hmm, that is nice. Leaning into the hand caressing my hair as my eyes open and I see… Pru!

"AAuuguhggh!" I throw myself at the other side of the bed, still in the haze of sleep, but I completely miss and hit the floor with a thump in a tangle of bedsheets. Groaning, I sit up to see her craziness hasn't moved and is watching me with a smile.

"My poor boy, I didn't mean to startle you. I haven't seen you in so long that I wanted to spend some time with you. You sleep so late though, I was beginning to worry that something might have happened to you. So I came in to check and you looked so sweet sleeping that I couldn't help but come over and smooth your hair back out of your eyes. I never meant to startle you, no, no. Not my sweet boy."

Oh good grief, it is so early for this level of crazy. Grabbing my sheet and holding it securely around my waist, I stand, "Yes. That's all very interesting, but I am going to need you to leave the room now. I need a shower and you should go have breakfast. Or do whatever it is you do this early in the morning."

"Oh, well, usually I try to follow Fate so I can see when she betrays you, but she hasn't come out of her room yet this morning. I guess she had a late night, I thought I saw some of your guards sneakily walking away from the area earlier. Maybe that has something to do with it?"

I feel my shoulders tighten as my head tips to one side. Adrenaline courses through my veins even as I remind myself that Pru cannot be trusted in regards to Fate. "Out Pru. NOW."

She pouts and says, "Not till you call me mom. I hate it when you use my name. It is so rude!"

I can't stop my eyes from rolling over this, "Fine, MOM. Get. Out. Now." I point at the doorway in case she 'forgets' which one. But she smiles like the sun came out and glides out of my room, shutting the door behind her.

Sitting on the bed, I check the door one more time before I let go of the sheet to put my elbows on my knees and cradle my head in my hands. I always thought karma was utter bullshit, but now, now I wonder if that bitch has noticed me. Rubbing my eyes I stand, lifting my feet higher to free them from the sheets I head for my bathroom and a much needed shower. As I set the shower to the right temperature, my mind wanders back to Fate. Did she have someone in her rooms last night? That was the only big rule I set, that she not have anyone else here. Stepping into the hot spray, I can feel my muscles relax and my senses begin to wake up. I'll just give Fate a good sniff. I should be able to tell whether or not she has had sex recently from that. My nose was very sensitive before I was turned, now I can smell the coffee brewing in the kitchen downstairs and across the house from here in my shower. Yes, that's what I'll do. Just give a sniff near her and that should tell me. But she probably didn't. She wouldn't. Shaking my head at my ridiculousness, I grab the shampoo. I need to get this shower done so I can go downstairs and reassure myself because obviously good old mom isn't the only lunatic here. I can't believe she was in my room! Yuck! Finishing up with rinsing off the soap, I turn the taps off, loathe as I am to do so. I look over at my towel bar on the wall outside the shower and no towel. What the hell? No one should have been in here — oh, no. Please tell me she isn't. I step forward and peek around the wall. There in my bathroom is Pru, holding out my fucking towel. Snarling, I tell her, "Drop the towel and get out!"

She bursts into tears but does not leave as she screams, "You don't even want your own mother around you at all! I should go throw myself off the roof! That would show you!"

Oh, for fuck's sake, "Give me the damn towel." She quiets immediately and hands over the towel. I wrap it around my hips, tucking the end in as securely as possible, and step out from behind the wall. "Throwing yourself off the roof isn't going to teach me anything, but it will teach you about how much healing can hurt. Because it hurts the whole damn time. Now get out of my bathroom—" she opens her mouth to shriek and I hold up a hand, "NO! Do not start that or I will banish you from the house entirely."

Paling Pru says, "You wouldn't!"

"I would. This is my house and the new rule is that you do not come in my bedroom or my bathroom without an invitation from me! Period! Now get out. I need to get dressed."

She reaches toward my towel saying, "Oh well I don't care about that, I saw you when you were born, go ahead."

Grabbing the tucked end to hold it in place, I tell her, "I do care. Don't make me tell you again to get out of my room."

She crosses her arms and pouts, but stumps her way to my bedroom door. She looks back to see if I am watching before she opens the door and steps out, leaving the damn thing open. I walk over and close it, hitting the lock while I am at it. In my closet I throw on a pair of dark gray slacks with a lighter gray silk button-up shirt, the jacket to match completes the outfit. Grabbing socks from the drawer, I slip them on and slide my shoes on over them. I give myself a once over in the full-length mirror standing in the corner. This is how a man with power should dress.

Fourteen

Stepping out of my room, I look both ways in the hall, but Pru is nowhere to be found. I sigh in relief. The bathroom incident was just too much. My shoulders give an involuntary shake as though trying to rid myself of the feeling of her being in the bathroom with me, while I was naked. There is just so much wrong with that, beginning with her being my reincarnated mother and ending with I am in love with her adopted sister. Looking at each end of the hall again, I close the door to my bedroom behind me and head toward Fate's room. I completely understand why she has it shielded all the time now. I knock on her door and wait, but I don't hear any movement from inside. After a moment I try the doorknob but am prevented from touching it by the shielding she has set.

I start downstairs, running into Rico on the way. He catches me up on the goings on of the house so far this morning, with the exception of the time that Pru disappeared, they aren't sure exactly where she went then. I fill him in on where exactly she went and to his credit; he has a great poker face. Not even his eyes gave him away. What gave him away was how quickly he excused himself to go discuss with Rico how best to deal with that. I feel certain they will work on the problem, after they laugh at my expense for the next half hour.

I head for the kitchen by way of the dining room, no Fate. I know she must be in the library, so I have cook make a tray with a carafe of coffee and some cherry scones. The tray readied, I take it and head for the library. As I draw near and slow to check the door for shielding Fate calls out, "Come in Charles, I opened the door for you."

I smile with pleasure that she chose to invite me in, however she was able to tell I was en route. How was she able to tell? She waves her hand at the doorway after I pass through without even looking up from her book. I set the tray on the table next to her and make my own coffee, taking a scone as I retreat to the chair across from her. I sip my coffee and watch in silence as she struggles to ignore the scents from the coffee and the scones. The way her nose twitches gives her away. I watch as she caves and sets her book aside.

Everyone has a tell. It doesn't matter who they are, everyone has a tell. Most people have a multitude of tells, different depending on what they are trying to hide. Fate, she has a few that I have found so far. When she is attempting to resist a food or similar, her nose twitches as she delights in the scents. When she tells part of the truth or lies outright, her eyes stray. Omission causes the same behavior. Now that I think about it, she has had that tell every time we spoke about witchcraft. I wonder…

"Thank you, Charles. I came in here last night when I couldn't sleep and I was so caught up in reading that I completely missed breakfast this morning."

She is so begrudging in that thank you that I can't help but chuckle, "How has your morning been Fate?"

She eyes me as if trying to decide whether or not I actually want to know, shrugs and says, "It's been a good morning. Pru has been happily absent, though I did notice the guards seemed to be searching for something this morning."

I groan, "Yes. They were searching for Pru. She disappeared on them because she came to watch me while I slept and smooth my hair back." A shudder ripples through me at the memory of her hand on my head as I woke up.

For her part, Fate snorts a couple times, trying not to laugh before she sets her coffee down and laughs, covering her mouth with her hands.

This is the first time I have seen her really laughing, she is stunning. Her eyes sparkle with a dark light and as she moves her hands away from her mouth, her smile is everything. "That isn't even the worst part. When I finished my shower, she was in my bathroom holding my towel! I get my towel back and tell her to leave so I can dress and she *tries to take the towel*. Telling me it is fine, she has seen me naked before. It is not fine! There is nothing ok about this."

By the time I have finished my tale of woe, Fate has fallen over on the couch, laughing and slapping a thigh as she holds her fist to her gorgeous mouth. There are tears streaming from her eyes and she is out of breath from laughing so hard. I would take the discomfort of this morning a thousand times over if I could keep making her laugh like this. She is calming down now, her breaths deepening as she returns to an upright position.

Still wiping the tears from her face she says, "Oh goodness Charles, I haven't laughed like that in so very long. Thank you." Sipping her coffee she asks, "Now that I am through laughing, are you okay? While it is hilarious from over here, I feel certain it was very disconcerting from your point of view."

My heart swells that she is concerned for me, "Yes, I am okay. I am not happy about Pru's incursions to my personal space, but I am okay. How are you holding up? I know you shield the library while you are here and your room, even when you are not in it, is that hard on you? Do you shield yourself when you aren't in here?" She looks away to the window. What doesn't she want to share? "Fate, you can tell me anything. I am not going to be mad at you. I am well aware that you have a phone and have likely called people to let them know you are well. I fully support that."

She looks at me with narrowed eyes, "Fine. No, it doesn't take anything to maintain the shields because my magical affinity is with air. Witches don't lose their power for becoming vampires Charles, we become a whole other creature and that much more dangerous for the added abilities. So I use magic to shield. Shielding is not the talent I was granted with vampirism, that talent is that I can feel where every soul is for quite some distance around me. As well as what they are generally doing. The people that live behind you spend an inordinate amount of time watching your house. You may want to look into that."

My jaw is hanging open, I know it is, but the commands just don't seem to be reaching it. When I manage to get it to shut my jaw snaps shut like a trap and the clack of my teeth meeting is fairly audible. She didn't lose her magic? How is that even possible? I thought, well, wrong apparently. My mind spins with this information. Holy shit, if she hadn't taken away her sister's powers, we would have a crazy vampire Pru running around with magic. "Remind me again, what exactly was the reason you took your sister's powers away?"

Fate pales, "I took her powers away because she had been mind-raping me for years and when I found out she was doing that to everyone, I couldn't let it go on. No one should have to go through that." I watch closely for any of her tells, and there is nothing but a slight tremor in her hands, as if she were reliving a frightening experience.

"Can you tell me about it?"

She grimaces, "What do you want to know?"

"How did you know she was in your head?"

"It feels like fingers combing through your mind. There is a feeling like something is inside you that doesn't belong."

"Is there a way to fight against it?"

"Yes, but it hurts. Every time. You shield your mind. That is roughly just you envisioning whatever type of shield you feel most confident with and maintaining it as she hammers at your fucking skull trying to force her way in."

She looks haunted and pale at this point, "One more question, how long had she been abusing you that way?"

She looks directly at me, her eyes so dark and cold, "Since her powers came in at the age of seven."

It is a struggle to keep my face composed as Fate turns to stare out the window. Thirty-four years of her sister invading her mind as she pleased, bashing her way in if Fate wouldn't cooperate. How the hell is Fate not insane? Why would Pru's parents allow this? I mean, what did they gain from it? Fate is the least likely to go fuck shit up person that I have ever met. I don't understand that. What I do understand is that Pru should never have her powers back. And I am not very sure that anyone should be able to do such things, ever. Fate looks so sad, I think we need a change of subject.

"My father seems interested in Pru, even if she is

crazy. What do you think of the idea that I convince him to woo her and take her on a very extended vacation?"

She looks over in surprise, "What?"

"My father. He seemed interested still in my mother and his eyes lingered on Pru, I think we could saddle him with the problem. Maybe."

She chuckles, "I don't think that's how it works Charles."

"It was an idea."

Fifteen

It is strange how comfortable I feel with him, even when it feels a bit like I am betraying Devon by enjoying time with Charles. It wouldn't be this way if we could all be friends. I feel Pru striding through the house in this general direction, "Pru seems to be heading this way, she is probably looking for you."

He groans, lifts his feet into the chair and leans so he can't be seen from the open doorway. I watch as Pru comes within a few feet of the door and stops, nose raised like a bloodhound. Turning her head this way and that, she stops, pointed at the library doorway. She looks me in the eye and runs at the seemingly open doorway. Knowing she is a vampire and isn't going to be terribly injured, I sip my coffee as she hits the barrier at a dead run, bouncing off it like a rubber ball. I hear her land in the hall, and she is immediately back up and stopping her run a hairsbreadth from the shield. She glares at me for a time while I sip my coffee and watch. Finally she asks, "Where is my boy?"

"Where is your what?"

"My Charles. Where is my Charles?" She drags her nails down the barrier over and over like she can't really stop herself.

I chuckle, "He isn't yours, even if he is the son of your soul. I have no idea where he is, in case you hadn't noticed, I am a prisoner here. Find him yourself."

If she weren't a vampire, I think she would have had a stroke right there in the doorway. Instead, she screams obscenities at me, some of which were quite shocking. I hadn't ever heard those! I see her guards Rico and Benny standing behind her, well behind her. Rico gives me a nod and I tip my head to him. He rolls his eyes and I have to sip my coffee to hide the smile. For her part, Pru hasn't even noticed this by play. Charles is sipping his coffee, eyes on the world outside the window. He really is a handsome sort.

The polar opposite of Devon's dark, brooding, slightly dangerous look. The danger emanating from Devon is all a front though, and anyone that takes the time to really notice him will know that pretty quickly. He is all muscles and grim face and ever-watchful, then he touches a book with the most care I have seen in a person. His caution with the books is surpassed only by the tenderness in his gaze when he looks at me.

Oddly enough, I have caught a similar gaze in Charles' eyes. His is tinged with some ferocity, I don't know the reason for that. Charles is blonde and blue-eyed and pale, he fits the typical vampire mold in a way that Devon and I will never fit. I look up from my seeming study of my coffee to Pru. Still in the doorway screaming her head off. She still looks like she could be Charles' mother. Her skin is pale like his, though her eyes are so light a blue they look white in some lights. I wonder if her soul was trying to be recognized by him if he ever saw her?

Rico has begun to dance behind Pru, the funniest moves he has. I am trying to keep my face composed, but it is difficult, he has moves. Even Benny cracks a smile as Rico rides an imaginary horse in circles around him. Then Pru starts in on yelling at me about how much our parents hated and feared me. My face freezes and even Rico stops playing. I wave a hand to send the door slamming shut in her face, and I set the sound barrier as well.

"Are you okay, Fate?"

I look up at Charles, "As okay as I will ever be with this. It will never be easy having the hate of people that were supposed to be your parents thrown in your face even as you wonder why your actual parents gave you up."

Charles nods, his lips pressed together. "May I ask you some more questions about your sister and what happened?"

My jaw clenches. This is the last thing I want to talk

about. Eyeing him, I ask, "What do you want to know? I am not saying I will answer, but maybe you do need a little more information if you are going to be taking care of her."

"I would like to know a little more about what she did to you and what caused you to take away her powers? Has she always been a little off because of your parents, or was there a thing that broke her brain?"

Sigh. Of course. He needs to know these things, but damned if I want to talk about them. Deep breath and unclench all the muscles.

I feel Pru walking back up to the door of the library and pressing her ear up to the door in an attempt to hear Charles in here. "Fine. Since she is actively at the door trying to listen in and obviously going to become more of a problem for you, I will answer your questions. No, Pru was not always so far out there. She was pretty normal as a small child, though our parents made her meaner and more entitled. She was pretty much the average selfish, entitled, white girl growing up; only she had an edge because she could read minds. That made retaliation next to impossible for most people. Any teacher or supervisor that thought to reprimand her would suddenly develop a raging migraine. She would swear everyone was just jealous of her, but I knew it was a lie and she hated me for not believing her. So aside from being an awful person, no, she wasn't crazy then."

I feel Pru scratching at the shield. While she won't ever get through, it is annoying. I set the outer shield to be covered with tiny needles of air. I swear I feel the wind laughing. A sip of my coffee and I continue, "If anything could be said to have broken her brain it would be when her son was stillborn and then her husband left her because he blamed her for the baby's death. It was utter crap. She would no more have hurt that baby than she would have stopped breathing. That baby meant the whole world to her. Her husband was trash, she wouldn't have been really sad about him leaving. But the fact that he walked out on her within days of her giving birth to a stillborn child, that broke her. Not so much him leaving, even then.

Just the timing of it and the way he blamed her added to the loss of her baby. She blamed herself too. She was certain there was something she could have done better or more of or something, and the child would have lived. But there was nothing that could have been done. As it was, she barely survived. There was no blame to be laid anywhere. She seemed to have healed after some years, but I think now that it was just on the surface."

Another sip of my coffee as I watch Charles process all I have told him so far. Pru is still outside the library, but she isn't touching the shield anymore. "As for the issue with her powers, well. That grew worse over the years. I thought for a very long time that I was the only one whose mind she invaded on a regular basis. She would mentally attack me if I did not just let her have at my mind. She was never gentle in my mind either. It seemed to make her happy to cause me pain as she strip mined my thoughts and experiences. I hated her for it, even though she was my sister.

I did learn how to block her and I frequently did, but she made that painful as well. Battering at my shields until I wanted to attack her. I had no idea that she was sifting through other people's minds as well until I watched the videos from my husband. He told his girlfriend in one of the videos that Pru knew things she shouldn't and that was how I knew for sure. Luckily, I had taken precautions already, or my team would have been seriously injured. When I asked Griselda for a spell to stop the incursions, she gave me two spells.

One to protect my mind from all mind readers and another for taking away the powers of a witch. The first spell is easy and quick, and since we thought it highly probable that she would be furious and go after those around me, we cast it on everyone. When I got home from having watched the videos, she had been to my house. While she couldn't get into their minds, they could feel it when she attacked. We got out the second spell. There were warnings with that one. The spell came directly from Persephone. To cast it felt like you were burning the flesh from your hands and arms. If you were casting it for jealousy or some other specious reason, the spell would turn on the casters."

Charles eyes have gone round at this point and his mouth is hanging just a little, "We cast the spell and the warnings were not false. It was viciously painful to cast. Once it was done Pru's behavior managed to become worse before she left, after I invited her in to talk to me. I hadn't seen her since until she showed up here. Her behavior has gotten worse, but I cannot be sure how much worse as most of what she presented us with was a lie."

Charles shakes his head and sets aside his now very cold coffee, "I see why you didn't want to talk about it. I know this was the cliff notes version but, wow. I feel like we can safely say that Pru's condition was pretty bad before she had her memories restored and became a vampire. I don't know what that will mean for any chance of a recovery going forward, but she has something humans usually don't have, the gift of time. She can take a hundred years or so to heal, and she will still have plenty of life to live ahead of her. Are you ok though? Having been through all these things, do you need a shoulder to cry on or someone to talk to?"

"Charles, while that is possibly one of the nicest senti-ments you have expressed since I met you, I'm fine. Really. For whatever reason, I didn't take everything in and lose parts of myself to it. I appreciate the asking though. For now, all this talk of sad things has made me very tired. I think I would like to go lie down now. I will leave the shield up here, no one will be able to enter until you have left the room. Stay as long as you like."

Sixteen

FATE

Leaving the library, I head for the stairs, daydreaming of a nice warm bubble filled bath in that enormous tub. Since I was turned the temperature hasn't been an issue, but bathing feels nicer. It is an odd perk, but I'll take it. I reach the top of the stairs and Pru appears in front of me. She attacks me and we fall together down the stairs. Though I was shielded already I manage to throw a shield around her as well as we tumble ass over kettle. Shielded or not, hitting the floor at the bottom of the stairs is no picnic.

I kick Pru back away from me, while I have her still shielded, and then I let her drop to the floor like the rotten potato she is lately. I start working to sort myself out while keeping my shielding in place.

Pru screams, "Did you see that? She tried to kill me!"

Rico chuckles as he says, "Doesn't look like she is very good at it."

I look over to Pru and I can't help but smile, Rico is great with the one liners. She doesn't appear to agree.

Her face has grown more red, and she is hollering, "I want my son out here this instant! He needs to know what she is trying to do with all her lies and schemes. How could you, Fate? Trying to kill your own sister? Maybe our parents were right to fear you. Maybe they could see the kind of murderous bitch you would become one day."

I raise an eyebrow at her as I stand. Apparently her desire to have me away from Charles had overridden her memory of the fact that he is holding me prisoner here. I don't even know what to say to her at this point, so I send a whisper in to Charles, "It would be best if you step out here, please."

Rico, Benny, and I just watch as Pru stomps back and forth, cracking tiles left and right. Her tantrum would be a thing of beauty, were it not so far away from reality. Even the guys appear impressed. Charles steps out of the library then, I watch as the shield drops around him and the sound of Pru's epic tantrum hits him. His eyes widen and he scans the room, finally noticing us standing off to the side. Unfortunately for him, Pru noticed him about that time. Standing in front of the door to the library, I had recently told her that he was not in.

She looks back at me, eyes narrowed, "He wasn't in the library? And what room is it that he just left?" Her voice rises with each word and her face is so red I wonder if it is possible for vampires to have a heart attack.

She runs over to Charles and throws herself in his arms saying, "Oh my darling boy, she tried to kill me! She just hates me so much. First she tells me that you aren't in the library and then she attacks me at the top of the stairs. I'm telling you, our parents were right when they thought she would grow to be evil. Just look at her! She's so dark-skinned, after all the effort my parents went to in order to give her the gift of beauty. She just threw it all away to show off the evil that lives inside her."

Charles extricates himself from Pru, "Are you quite sure this is how it went?"

"Of course I am, dear boy. I watched over her for years at my parents' request. I watched as she whored about, breaking hearts left and right. Watched her as she used and manipulated Charlie after he was kind enough to marry her so that her tarnished reputation wouldn't be such a burden on our family. I watched as she celebrated his death, the one that she pushed him to, and she kept his inheritance from the one that should have had it to begin with."

Charles gives her a confused look, "If she was his wife then she is the one that was supposed to inherit? I don't understand what you are getting at here."

"Oh, she was his wife, but in name only by then. He was planning to leave her. He had fallen deeply in love with a woman named Amalia, and he intended for her to have all of it. But Fate just couldn't be a good girl and die before Charlie did. Nooo, she had to be just lucky enough for him to die two days after he paid the assassin."

"Wait, so you knew about all this and you never said anything to her? You spent years spying on your sister for your parents?" Charles looks over at me, "How did you manage to come out of this with so little apparent damage?"

Seventeen

FATE

Unfortunately for Charles he didn't recognize the warning signs of my temper.

My eyes were already narrowed and my jaw had been tight for long minutes now, as I attempted to keep it shut with willful gulps of silence. It wasn't working. Pru's suggestion that I should have laid down and died to be out of Charlie and his girlfriend's way absolutely infuriated me.

"How dare you Pru." My eyes follow her as she jumps behind Charles, I feel certain she was trying to goad me into showing Charles my temper, but so what. Let him be scared. Let them all be scared. "How fucking dare you tell my story, MY STORY, and twist it so far it is near unrecognizable. Our parents, as you are calling them now, though they were only your parents, were abusive as hell. All the things you did, the continual mind rape, the way you siphoned information from our friends! I may not be an innocent in this world but I have never done half the damage fucking someone as you have intentionally done every day of your life!"

I slam shields around Pru when she starts looking like she wants to apparate and I stalk my way toward her. Charles does me the favor of stepping out from between us. "You conspired with my husband to have me murdered!" I see the surprise flit across her face, "Oh, that's right, I wasn't supposed to find out. Well, unfortunately for you, Charlie made tapes. He ratted you out to his girlfriend. And he knew. He knew you were picking things out of his brain, even if he didn't know quite how you were managing it. He warned his girlfriend, who did not get the memo, fortunately for me." I am right up in her face now and her eyes are wide and scared. "How you feel right this minute? That is how you need to feel when you see me coming! I am done trying to be nice to you! I will treat you as you deserve from now until eternity. No more Pru. You steer clear of me or I will be the last person you see on this planet."

Pru is blubbering and shivering now, I turn away from her in disgust. I hear Charles clear his throat off to the side and I turn to him. He says, "I don't know if you are aware of it but you appear to be on fire…"

I hold my hands out in front of me, Holy Hera, I am.

There are blue flames all over me. Fuck. How do I get this to stop? I close my eyes and draw in some slow, deep breaths. Concentrating on visualizing the flames dying down and disappearing. When I open my eyes again, the flames on my hands are gone. I look at Charles, "Are they all gone?"

He nods.

"Good. I am going to my room. I will release that idiot when I get in there."

Eighteen

FATE

I stomp my way up the stairs. I am still pretty damned mad. Fuck her. Fuck those shitty, racist assholes that adopted me and then decided I needed to be whiter to better fit their image. Stepping into my room, I slam the door and release Pru. Opening the drawer with my phone in it, I grab my phone and take it to the bathroom. Turning on the taps, I pour in a bunch of the eucalyptus smelling bubble bath they put in here for me and dial Natasha and Memré.

Once they are both on the phone, I start sobbing the whole sorry tale of what just happened out to them. "I don't know how much longer I can take this." The two have made encouraging noises up to this point, as they waited for me to get enough out that I could calm down. "I was on fire. I was so mad that there were actual flames on me. Where did I get fire from? I shouldn't have fire. What is going on here?"

Memré speaks first, "I have a pretty good idea of which place you are in based on his bills. We could come and get you, sweetie. You don't have to stay there."

Natasha counters, "I don't know about that. Grams has been reading the cards, and she seems to think Fate needs to get Charles on her side. That he needs to be the one to bring her home. She says the current cycle will end very badly if she doesn't."

"What do you mean he needs to bring her home? Nat, what the fuck? We know where she is, and what is the worst that could happen?"

Natasha sighs, "That's just it, she can't see any farther than that. Which is weird because usually she can, but this time it just goes to everything bad if we go get her while it goes to too many paths if he brings her home. She has to stay the course here, even if it is really awful right now. Which it sounds like it is…"

I nod, "Yes, but mostly because Pru is here. It really wasn't the worst thing ever before that. I missed everyone, Devon especially, but this was a nice place to be. Now my sister is here and so awful that I got mad enough to catch on fire. I'm a little scared."

Memré sighs, "Of course you are, that is scary. Being

frightened is a really normal reaction. But you are stronger than a little fear. So how about this, Nat's Grams says Charles has to be the one to bring you home, but he doesn't know that. Threaten him a little. Tell him we know where you are, it is completely true. Tell him the only thing keeping us from taking you back is you. Also true, mostly. True enough that you can say it and not be lying. Maybe that little bit of leverage will help you to convince him to bring you home. Or I could take all of his money. I have control of most of it right now. I left him control of some of it for now. I'll probably give it all back when he brings you home."

"Oh geez, well. I guess Charles asked for that. I will tell him what you said, I am going to keep quiet on the money part though. He can find that out on his own. Hopefully, you left him plenty to get Pru all the help she could possibly need because she needs a ton of it."

Memré laughs, "Yeah, there is still plenty. Even for specialists. He is really loaded from all that drug money."

Natasha asks, "Is he going to get her some help?"

"I don't know. I am going to advocate for it, but I have no idea whether he will listen or not. I should probably get off the phone, I need to get myself out of this tub and get some rest. Today has been weird."

We all say our goodbyes, and I set the phone down on the shelf that runs around the entire tub. The water is warm and has soothed muscles that I didn't realize were locked up. I do eventually drag myself out of the tub and dry off. Back in my room, I turn off my phone and tuck it away back in its drawer. A wave of my hand sets the shield around it again. I throw on some jammies that were in here when I arrived and crawl into the bed. My eyes are heavy and as soon as I lay my head on the pillow, everything goes away.

Nineteen

FATE

I wake to the sound of knocking on my door. I fumble with the blankets and stumble my way across the room to open the door, careful to keep myself on this side of the shield because who knows, it could be Pru out there. Peering through my hair before I realize I can shove it back out of my face, I see Charles. "I was sleeping, Charles. What do you want?"

He looks like he is still bothered by everything that happened earlier and I can't blame him; I know I am. Running a hand across the back of his neck he says, "I want to talk to you about…" he waves his hands in either direction, "all of this."

I nod, step back further and alter the shielding so he

can walk through for now. "Come in Charles, we can sit in front of the fire." One of the nicer perks of vampirism is that night vision really is a thing, and I don't need any light to see where I am going. I turn on a lamp anyway once I get to the seating area in front of the fireplace. As gilded cages go this place is nice. Charles kneels in front of the gas fireplace and gets it going before he takes the seat across from me. I pull up my legs and cross them in the chair. It is big and cushy. I love it. I want one for my bedroom at home.

Charles stares into the fire for a bit. I wait in silence because I am always slow to wake up. Still looking into the fire, Charles says, "I brought in a doctor."

"For Pru? Oh, that is wonderful. I am really glad to hear that. Is the doctor a vampire too or a witch or something else?"

He nods, "The doctor is a vampire. I wanted someone as strong as she is, or stronger. Just in case. The first thing he did was to sedate her. After you left the room, she was pretty hysterical. Apparently watching flames crawl over your skin while you told her off was upsetting to her."

I look away now, "I never told her off before today. It wasn't my finest moment, that's for sure. But it was long overdue. She really has done a lot of things that are just awful. It's no excuse on my end, but that is my reason. I am glad she is sedated. Does he have any ideas about what is wrong with her?"

"Not yet. He said he wants to see what her baseline is. How she is normally. I gave him a rundown of the things I knew had happened. He is going to take all that into account. He said that he may notice some things that I wouldn't, just because he has been watching patients and training to notice little things that an untrained person would not. Being a vampire, he has access to many years more training than the average doctor. Especially since every so often he has to die and start over." He chuckles at that last part and I smile. He really does have a nice smile. Even when it is as wry as that one was.

Giving myself a mental shake, I don't need to be thinking about him like this; I steer myself back on course. "I need to change the subject, not that I don't want to be kept apprised of what is happening with Pru. I do. But we need to talk about this whole situation that has me here."

Twenty

FATE

Charles looks back into the fire, his jaw set. Oh good grief, he's going to be like that. "Charles. Charles, I need you to look at me. Not sulk at the fireplace." I wait until he looks over at me. His eyes tell a different story as they regard me heavy with longing. I want to go sit in his lap and comfort him, but I can't betray Devon like that. What is wrong with me? Is it Stockholm syndrome? Is that what this is? "Charles, don't look at me like that. I can't take it. I won't say that I don't feel anything for you, but the fact is that I won't betray Devon. Maybe there could be some arrangements made, but you have to make up with Devon. And you have to take me home."

I watched as his eyes lit up, dulled, and then sparkled. I

can't even imagine the kind of roller coaster his feelings must be on right now. "Devon is a pretty forgiving guy, and you two were friends once. Best friends, if I understand correctly. I think it would be good for both of you if you could make up, become friends once again. Plus, they know where I am. My friends are ready to come bust me out of here. The only thing holding them back is, well… Me."

Shock registers on his face at the last sentence. I guess it is a little weird sounding, but he doesn't know the rest of it. Because if Natasha had said nothing about Grams predictions I would have let them come get me earlier. I watch Charles turn things over in his mind before he speaks, "I can't let you go. Maybe I can make up with Devon, and I could even probably share you with him if you were ok with that. But I… I can't let you go. I don't know what changed between now and the last times you were here, but now I could no more stay away from you than I could—"

"I am not asking you to not be a part of my life, Charles. I am asking you to let the other people that are part of my life be part of my life. I was working to buy a larger house or grouping of houses when you kidnapped me. Something like a compound but without all the detrimental ideology or weapons cache."

Charles blushes and looks into the fire, "I may be overly concerned about being pushed out of your life right now." He stands and crosses the space between us to kneel in front of me, taking my hands in his he whispers, "I feel like my world will end if I don't keep you safe with me. I will give thought to taking you back to everyone else or them coming here, on one condition." His face is inches away from mine and I know I should move away, but it feels like there is a magnet inside him targeting me.

Struggling not to drift toward him, I panic as I realize he is drifting toward me, "What is the condition?"

His lips curve upward, like he knows what is going through my mind, "You don't send me away. Whatever happens between Devon and I, please don't send me away from you. It isn't really a condition, more of a request. Please don't send me away from you, Fate. I know I can't hold you hostage forever, but I would beg if it meant you would not send me away from you."

He is a breath away from my lips as he finishes pleading with me not to send him away. The electricity of attraction dancing between our bodies is nearly visible. It takes everything I have to lift my hands, still held by him, and push him back from me. "I won't send you away. At this point, I am not sure I could. I don't know how all this will work out. Do people do this? Do they have more than one love? Mate? Whatever? Is this a vampire thing? I am so confused. I know Devon and I are tied together, but it almost feels like we could be too. I don't understand any of this. For tonight, I need you to leave my room. I won't cheat on Devon, and doing anything right now would feel like that. Get thee from my sight, temptation."

Charles smiles at me and leans in, moving my hands away from his shoulders, and just before our lips meet he moves his face to the left and kisses my cheek. I exhale a shaking breath as he stands, and I notice the bulge in the front of his pants. He notices my attention on his package and grins. Taking care to slowly adjust himself into a more comfortable position as I watch, rapt. Then he puts his hands in his pockets and walks to the door, stopping to offer, "Pleasant dreams" before he opens the door and steps out of my room.

Pleasant dreams indeed. Devil man.

Charles

Stepping out of Fate's suite, I am overjoyed and horny. She said she wouldn't send me away though, and that makes me so happy. I can't recall a time when I have been this happy and this uncomfortable all at the same time. I am grateful that my suite is only a few steps down the hall and that Pru is safely sedated. A text hits my phone as I step in my room, and then another, and another. My phone is blowing up with texts. I pull it out of my pocket as I shut the door behind me. I wonder if I could convince Fate to place a shield over my room too? To prevent Pru from popping in when she pleases. Opening the messages, I see they are all from my accountants. They are all freaking out because my accounts have been taken over. They have lost access and don't know why, neither does the bank. I message them back to ask if it is all the accounts and they say no, there are three that are untouched. I tell them to hold off on doing anything about the ones they cannot access for the moment. Fate told me that her friends know where she is, I wonder if this has something to do with it? As that thought occurs to me, I message a second time and tell them to start new accounts in another name I keep on standby, just in case. All seem relieved at this, so I have to guess they wanted to ask but were afraid.

I strip off my clothes, tossing them in a basket. Walking into the bathroom, I realize I am still hard for Fate when my engorged shaft hits the counter, causing me to drop the phone still in my hands to grab myself with one hand and the counter with the other. The swelling doesn't abate even a little with the pain of smacking it into the counter. As the pain recedes I let go of myself and the counter, to go through the motions of my nightly hygiene. A few minutes later I crawl into bed, teeth and hair brushed. Laying on the back staring at the ceiling, I think of Fate and how she smelled of jasmine and sandalwood. My manhood, which had finally returned to a resting state, swells right back up. My sheets are tented over my hips and I am aching with the want of her. It's going to be a long night.

Twenty-One

FATE

I am just finishing dressing for the day when I feel the spell wash over me. Panic is my first reaction. I know Memré is pushing them to come get me now, but I believe Griselda when she says things have to be done a certain way. I snatch my phone out of the drawer and wait impatiently for it to boot up after I tap the button. It finally does and I unlock it, hitting the message button. I send out a group text, '*Do not come get me. I will be home soon. Give me a little more time.*' I set the ringer to silent and shield myself against any possible Pru attacks. Stepping out of my room I don't see her and checking the time on my phone I head for the dining room. Charles sees me enter and walks over to greet me, but instead of stopping a reasonable distance away, he invades my space. I keep backing away from him until I bump into the wall. He stops with our bodies just barely not touching and puts his lips next to my ear, "I ached for you all night." Then he turns around and walks back over to the spread laid out by his kitchen staff. I take a deep breath to try to calm my now racing pulse as my mind helpfully recalls the image of the bulge in his pants from last night.

Breathing semi-normally again, I walk over to load up my own plate as Charles takes his seat at the table. I load mine up with fresh fruit and a croissant. Sitting across from Charles, I tear off a piece of croissant and pop it into my mouth to keep it busy while I decide how to say this.

Charles stops that train of thought when he says, "Any ideas about why many of my accounts are no longer under the care of my accountants?"

I freeze, yes. Yes, I do have ideas. Crap. Swallowing the last of that bite, I say, "I, I do."

He nods, "I assumed as much. Will they return it when I bring you back?" He is studiously looking down at his plate as he carefully cuts his waffle into small, bite-sized pieces. I can't help but watch as he collects a piece onto his fork and carefully places it in his mouth. His lips close over the fork and pulls it from his mouth. Shaking my head, I realize I am staring, luckily before he did.

"I think they will. Most of it, at least?"

He nods again, "I can live with that. Now, I think there was something you wanted to tell me?"

I nod, my mouth full of strawberry. I swallow the berry

and say, "Yes. I felt my friends cast a spell to find me just a bit ago. I sent them a message to wait, to not come and get me but, I think we are running out of time for you to make a decision about taking me home."

"So they know exactly where you are and are following your instructions to not come get you yet?"

"Yes. For now. But it is only a matter of time before they grow tired of waiting and tell Devon where I am. He, he is not so amiable about this. I know he will be once I am returned, but for now… Well. What would you do?"

He shrugs, "Storm the castle. I see your point. I still need to think about this. If I am honest, I want to have you here and to myself for a little bit longer. I am selfish in that way. Your presence, your scent," he tilts his head back slightly and inhales through his nose, "I never knew how much I love the scent of jasmine and sandalwood. It has been a long time since I felt more than the desire for revenge. I want to soak up these feelings a little longer, even if it does mean I spend a lot of time readjusting so my pants are not tented out like a young boy. Your presence is like mana from the heavens and I have been starving for a long time." His blue eyes blazed as he spoke, and for my part I felt a pulsing in my core and a desire to moan with need. I really need to go home to Devon before I do something I will regret.

He is the second man I have ever wanted, like I want Devon. My mind, ever helpful, supplies me with a picture of me entangled with Devon and Charles; I feel a dampness between my legs. Charles sniffs the air lightly, then breathes in deeply through his nose and grins at me. Dammit. He can smell my arousal, how wonderful. Not.

"Just because I am aroused by pretty speeches doesn't change anything. You know that, right?"

He looks like the cat that stole the cream as he says, "I know. But I am happy to have aroused your lust simply talking to you." With that, he pops another bite of waffle into his mouth and chews with a smile. I roll my eyes at him, mumbling men under my breath. I know he can hear me, but I look down at my plate and work on eating my breakfast so I don't have to see that satisfied look on his face.

Twenty-Two

FATE

Charles asks, "Have you got your shields up Fate?" He sounds worried but I always have my shields up, I just had them pulled in closer since Pru is with her doctor.

I push them out since he asked and tell him, "Always. I just had them in closer earlier. Why?"

"Pru is coming. Drugged or not, we know how she reacts to you. I want you safe."

Pru walks in to the dining room then. Scanning the room, she sees Charles first and smiles at him. Her eyes move across the table and her face screws up into a scowl as she sees me. She marches over to be next to me and tries to spit at me. I am enraged and send it flying back into her face before I wrap her in air and moving a chair out from the table I slap her into it none too gently.

Charles is watching, wide-eyed, and I ask, "Dammit, am I on fire again?"

He shakes his head no and starts chuckling. The chuckles build into full-blown laughter and by the time he calms himself both of us are glaring at him. He wipes tears from his eyes saying, "Sorry, sorry. I couldn't help it."

Pru looks away from him and starts screaming nonsense at me. I do not have any patience for it and I slap a shield of silence over her just as the doctor comes stumbling into the room rubbing his head. I can smell the blood from the minor cut that was on his head and he looks annoyed. Very annoyed.

Doctor Z sees Pru and realizes she is shouting her head off even if he can't hear it. He looks over at me, "Say, that is a splendid trick. It is a shame I haven't the ability. You must be Fate. Very nice to meet you. Sorry about that, Charles, as you can tell, Pru hit me over the head. She's got an arm on her. Knocked me clean out for a bit. Hope she hasn't caused too much problem already."

Charles smiles at the doctor, "No, quite the opposite. Fate, can she hear us through your shield?" I shake my head no and he continues, "Oh good. She caused me a great bit of entertainment when Fate sat her down after she tried to spit in Fate's face."

Doctor Z sits down next to Charles saying, "She does seem to have a jealous fixation on Fate. I have rarely seen people so focused on a sibling in such a detrimental manner. That and her intense fixation on you as her son, she makes for a strange case. Fate, could you; do you have any ideas that you would be willing to share with me about why your sister is so jealously focused on your downfall?"

I nod, swallowing the bits of melon I had been feasting on and begin to tell him about our childhood. He nods and makes noises of discovery, but is mostly silent as I speak.

When I have finished he says, "That puts a different light on things. I feel like this break is more of a result of long-term, suppressed issues rather than that of recent events. The vampire mind is fascinating though and can often heal things like this given enough time and some aid." He looks at Charles, "This is what I suggest. What I think is likely to be the best and least traumatic route for her and everyone around her. I want to sedate her into an induced coma. This will give her subconscious mind time to work through things that she wouldn't ordinarily be able to work through because of the mania. While she is in this coma, we need to find a mind witch. A very good one that has experience with healing a fractured mind like Pru's. I know of a few that may be talented enough, and I will work to get in touch with them, if you agree to this plan of mine. However, I would not be averse to you finding any you thought would be capable. Is this course of treatment amenable to you both?"

I look to Charles and he raises his brows, I shrug and say, "It seems like the best idea I have heard so far. It would be nice to have her sedated so I am not constantly worrying about attacks and you don't have to worry about your mom trying to help you in the shower." My lips twist into a wry smile as he shivers and glares at me.

"I thought we weren't going to talk about that?"

"You're right, sorry. It is funny though."

Shivering again, Charles denies my statement, "No. There is nothing funny about that. It was incredibly disturbing." He turns to the doctor, "Yes, we both agree to it. Just be absolutely sure that the dosage is high enough to keep her out."

Doctor Z nods, "Yes. I will also need some other vampires to tend to her around the clock. I do not know of any that are nurses so, just some that can be trained in the care of Pru. I will come by daily to check on her, make sure her care is progressing well. But I have other patients to tend to and so cannot spend all my time here. They must be vampires, in case she wakes up. Sometimes they begin burning through the medication at a faster rate. We will put it in the blood we feed her, making it more likely to stay effective. But sometimes things happen."

"Of course Doctor Z, I have some people that we have kept trained in first aid sorts of things. Vampire first aid, that is. So they are good at setting bones and closing wounds, I think they would likely work."

I nod at the doctor, "You should definitely expect the unexpected with her. She is very resourceful."

Pru begins thrashing about, foaming at the mouth, and Doctor Z jumps up, saying, "Does she have a history of seizures?" He runs over to her and watches very closely as

I tell him no. He looks over at me, "Do not let her go. Keep her bound."

I laugh, "There was absolutely no chance of that happening."

We watch as the seizing cuts off like it never happened and Pru opens her eyes about halfway, looking at us without looking directly at us. I raise my brows because at this point I know she is faking it. I watch the doctor as he purses his lips while studying every little move she makes. He eventually looks over at me, "I sincerely doubt she has had a seizure. We will keep an eye on that, but the chances of a vampire, even a vampire that had seizures prior to being turned, having them as a vampire is astronomically low. Negative numbers low." He returns to his seat, shaking his head as he goes. "Your sister was treated as your parents' personal monitor for you and everyone else as soon as she began to develop powers, correct?"

"That is my understanding. Admittedly, I only found out recently about her monitoring everyone else. I thought it was just me, and I was unaware that she was reporting back to my parents all the time. I don't know anything about how harsh her coaching from them may or may not have been. I do know," I look over at Pru, "I know, well, about when she lost her baby." Charles looks to Pru with a sad smile on his face, luckily she is still feigning sleep or has accidentally fallen asleep. "It was not an easy pregnancy to begin with, and her husband made it more difficult. He was controlling and incredibly selfish. He was certain that she would have a boy to continue his line.

Labor started early and her baby was in fact a boy. But he was stillborn."

The doctor nods and makes sympathetic noises while Charles motions for me to go on with the story.

"When her husband arrived at the hospital, he was fresh from his girlfriend's house. His hair was mussed and there were stains in various places. He came in the room, told her it was her fault that his son died and then got knocked out by some strange invisible force." I look down at my plate for a moment, I know it is a tell but I don't care. It makes me want to laugh maniacally every time I talk about it. "Pru was crushed, and it took a really long time for her to stop chasing him and trying to convince him to give her another chance. It was heartbreaking to watch, but she did eventually get a lot of therapy and I thought she was getting herself together and moving on until she cracked and started behaving erratically. It only got worse from there."

Doctor Z nods, "That does give me some insight into what is happening with her. I would love to be able to talk to her parents?"

"Ah, well, they're dead. For quite a while now. I mean, I guess you could get someone to snatch their souls back from wherever they are but seems like a lot of work when they aren't likely to tell you much. Griselda might be able to tell you more about them. She knew them back in the day, but her opinion of them is not anything like favorable."

Waving that concern away Doctor Z says, "Probably

better if it is someone that didn't like them. More likely to tell me the good stuff. How can I get in touch with her?"

"If you will give me your number, I will have her give you a call. She likes to be choosy about who can call her and I respect that because I love her and because Griselda is dangerous. I want to live."

Laughing, he writes down his number on a scrap he pulled from his pocket and hands it to me. Then he says, "Fate, could you float her up the stairs? After I sedate her that is."

"Of course, whenever you like."

Standing, the good doctor pulls a syringe out of his pocket. Walking over to Pru, he carefully pushes the needle into her arm and presses the plunger. Pru starts to struggle but her struggles are brief and she is out quickly. The doctor nods at me and I stand, levitating Pru and following the doctor upstairs to Pru's quarters.

Twenty-Three

Leaving Pru's quarters, I head straight for my own. Inside, I throw up the sound shield within the outer shield and pull my phone out of the drawer. Turning it on, I hit the code and tap Devon's name in the contacts. He answers on the first ring, "Fate! Fate, baby, can we come and get you now? I miss you so much."

"I miss you too. Don't come get me just yet, I think I have him convinced to bring me home. There is one thing though…"

He growls, "And what is the one thing?"

"Would it be possible for you and him to be friends? He is just on the edge of bringing me home, he has kept his hands to himself all this time, and other than being kept away from you all this hasn't been a terrible place to be. But he says that he can't stand to be away from me."

Devon growls some more. It sends a shiver right to my very empty core, reminding me that it has been so long since I have been in his arms as he buries himself in me.

I let out a shaky breath, "You can't keep growling, it does things to me and you aren't here to do anything about it."

"I could be. I could swoop in and take you from him whether or not he likes it."

I smile, "I know. But Griselda said this is how it needs to happen. She is never wrong. If she says it, that is what has to happen. She doesn't often speak in absolutes either. I trust her, more than I ever did my parents or my sister. I need to do it this way, and I hope you can be okay with that."

Devon sighs, "Yes. I don't like it, but yes. I will trust in her for now. When do you think you can get him to bring you home? I need you."

There goes the entire core of me, clenching with need of him. "Mmm, you are killing me. Soon. Maybe later or tomorrow?"

"I think I can be ok with that. Especially if you come home tonight and we can take care of all this need built up between us. He and I are going to have to come to our own agreement once he brings you back, but then I am carrying you off and ravish you."

"Uuunnhh, I like that. The only thing I ask is that you two not try and kill each other. That would really delay the ravishing, and I could use a good ravishing. I need to go. I have to go be seen out and about or people start coming to check on me."

"All right, come home soon, love. The sooner the better. I miss you, I want you, I love you."

"I miss you, want you, and love you, my darling Devon. I will be home as soon as I can."

Twenty-Four

FATE

I wake the next morning, eager to find out what Charles has decided. I can only hope that he has decided to take me home, I don't want to do other than what Griselda instructed but I am really ready to go home. If he is going to be stubborn about things, then I may have to call her and ask her if it counts as him taking me home if I have him in the trunk.

Twenty minutes later I am dressed and ready to find Charles. I throw up a shield around me before I leave my room, just in case Pru is wandering about. Last thing I need is her attacking me unshielded. Opening my door, I peek around just to see if anyone is hanging about and step out after seeing no one, closing the door behind me. I hurry down the stairs and off to the dining room, relieved to find Charles is just serving himself from the buffet. I walk over and picking up a plate begin adding bits for my own breakfast. I keep an eye on Charles, trying to assess his state of mind without obviously watching him. He has his poker face on; I don't know if that means he is troubled or what. As I sit down the doctor comes in and sits down next to Charles, asking him, "When will your people be arriving?"

"They should be here within the hour. Some of the boys left to pick them up about an hour ago."

"Oh good, I have had a call and I need to be somewhere this afternoon." With that, he stands and fills his own plate. We pass our breakfast talking about various things and the doctor entertains us with tales of patients long dead and gone. Setting my plate in the bin for dirty dishes, I turn just as Charles steps up behind me, my nose just avoiding crashing into his chest. I inhale and oh sweet lady does he smell good! Swallowing, I step back and bump the cart. No where to go.

He smiles down at me and reaches around me to place his plate in the bin. Then he leans down, putting his lips next to my ear he whispers, "You smell delicious." A shiver runs through my body and my core clenches. He inhales deeply and steps away from me asking, "Would you come to the library and talk with me? I will have the staff bring us some tea or coffee, if you prefer?"

"Yes," I say shakily, clearing my throat to continue, "I would prefer coffee."

I head for the library while he enters the kitchen to put in our order. I sit down in my favorite spot and work to restore my equilibrium. He walks in and takes the chair across from me, smiling like the devil he is.

"Oh stop. You have an effect, congratulations. I am not going to act on that effect."

He grins wider, "I am just happy to have an effect."

I scowl at him, and one of the staff walks in with a tray. They set it down on the table between us, ask if there is anything else we would like and upon getting a no, they exit the room closing the door behind them. I lean forward and pour myself a cup of coffee, adding cream and sugar till it reminds me of Devon. I wait while Charles prepares his tea in much the same manner as I did my coffee.

After he has a sip I ask him, "Have you made your decision?"

"You are still in contact with Devon, correct?" I nod and he continues, "Have you spoken with him about this?"

"I have."

"What are his thoughts on this? On my need to stay near you? Has he planned my demise yet?"

I laugh, "No, he hasn't, actually. He isn't overjoyed by it, but he is agreeable. He wants me home. Beyond that, he wants to have a talk with you, I won't speculate on the topics. I know the two of you have a long history between you."

"Is he prepared to have me there, or for all of you to come here? I was not kidding about needing to have you near."

"I haven't asked him, but you could ask him yourself if you took me home. The only thing I can guarantee is that you will not be attacked for bringing me home. The rest, we can work out. I was going to buy a larger home, perhaps we could all live there. I am not entirely sure I want to be on constant guard against Pru and living in the same house as her would require that. Even if she is drugged right now. She has a long road ahead of her. We don't know how much of that road she will spend still hating me, trying to kill me. For all we know, her seeing me regularly could be spectacularly bad for her healing."

Charles' brow furrows, "You have a point. Perhaps I should get her set up in some sort of private care home." He shakes his head, "I had already decided if I am honest. I knew I was going to take you home because I have a hard time saying no to you. Getting to know you has only made the craving for you deeper. Once you started asking to go home, the only reason I didn't immediately take you home is that I was near paralyzed with the fear that I would never be in your presence again." He stares deeply into his tea after his confession. Looking back up he says, "I need to tell you, I love you Fate. I don't know how or why it happened, but it did and there is no getting away from it for me now. I can live with you being with someone else, I am a patient man if nothing else. But I cannot live without you in my life."

He holds up a hand when I open my mouth to speak, "I don't expect a declaration of love from you or an explanation of why you don't. I know you are with Devon and you

were in love with him for well over a century now. I just
need to be part of your life and for you to be part of mine. I
won't expect anything more of you, and I won't pressure
you beyond the odd, entertaining opportunity to make you
blush like you did in the dining room."

"I did not blush! I don't blush!"

He chuckles, "Maybe you didn't when you were glamoured white but you certainly do now. Your cheeks lit up
like a beacon."

"I do not blush. You are delusional, sir." I cross my
arms over my chest and look away to keep him from
seeing the smile playing at the edges of my lips.

He laughs outright, "Whatever you say, princess."

An hour later I am outside, purse in hand, standing in front
of a black Geneva Edition Denali. The windows are
blacked out, but Rico and Benny get out of the front and
walk over.

Rico says with a laugh, "Hey there princess. The boss
says we get to help guard you, instead of the crazy lady.
You not gonna set us on fire, are you?"

I narrow my eyes at them, "No. It would seem the only
thing I set on fire is myself. But I am getting real good at
making annoying sounds go away, want a demonstration?"
Benny starts laughing as Rico backs away with his hands
up in supplication. I laugh too, letting him relax, knowing
that I was joking. The door behind me opens and Charles

emerges with three bags; two computer/briefcase types and a garment bag. He hands the garment bag over to Benny who, still chuckling, takes it to the back of the Denali and opening the hatch, hangs it up in the back. Rico smiles at me and opens the door for Charles and I. Charles waves a hand in the direction of the Denali saying, "Ladies first." I climb in and move to the seat on the passenger side, Charles takes the seat next to me and Rico closes the door. Charles sets his bags gently on the floor and leans them against the seat across from him. He turns to me and asks, "Are you excited to go home?"

"I am. Your hospitality has been top notch beyond the kidnapping thing, but I really miss my family."

"The others that live with you. How did you meet them?"

"Well, I grew up with Natasha. Billy is one of Devon's friends. The rest, they are my bodyguards. I met them during the hiring process. They are all special to me, though. Every one of them has been more like family to me than mine ever was, and that, that is important to me in a way I didn't realize until I had all of them."

Nodding, Charles makes an encouraging noise, asking, "Was your family never family to you?"

"No, not that I can recall. Not that I actually realized until I was much older that the way they treated me was not how family treats family. Natasha was always one of my best friends and that hasn't changed beyond I appreciated her more and more as time went by. The rest of them treating me like I matter to them, beyond a paycheck. I didn't quite know what to do at first." I wipe away a tear trying to creep down my face, "My family never made me feel like that."

Charles covers my hand on the armrest and gives it a squeeze while I look out the window and try to compose myself.

A few quick minutes later we pull up to the house, and I am overjoyed to see it. I contain myself and turning to Charles I put a shield over him, just in case. Devon definitely feels a way about things, and I don't want him to do anything any of us will regret. I start to open my door and recall that Charles was not the only threat before I left, so I shield myself as well. Getting out of the Denali, I lead the way with Charles, Rico, and Benny following closely behind.

Stopping at the door, I turn and say, "Whatever the reaction is here, I need you all to behave. I will get it sorted. You just have faith in me and know that I will not let any of you come to harm."

Benny and Rico start laughing, "Boss, what does she need us for?"

Without turning to face them he says, "She needs you for the ones that aren't her family."

The boys stop laughing at that and I shrug, turning round and digging my keys out of my purse. Just as I start to put my key in the lock Billy opens the door. I look up and smile. He throws his arms open and wraps them around me, lifting me off my feet in a hug. He spins around, whooping for all he is worth that I am home. His spinning has brought us further into the house, Charles and the boys followed, Rico shut the door behind them. As Billy sets me down I hear the sound of many people coming toward us at a fair rate of speed, Billy hears it too and shoves me in front of him so that I am between him and the mob headed our way. Everyone in the house right now has come to see me, and my heart is overflowing with happiness to see them all again. Devon waits at the back of the crowd, letting everyone else greet me before he grabs me up in a bear hug and kisses me for all he's worth. He is worth so much; I need dry panties. Remembering that we have an audience, we disengage and I look around to see that my bodyguards have created a wall of bodies between the two groups of people. Still holding Devon's hand, I say, "That isn't needed guys. Really. Charles brought me back of his own free will. He isn't going to kidnap me ever again, right Charles?"

He nods, "I promise, I will not kidnap her nor allow her to come to any harm because of me. I am not reformed by any means, but I am under her spell the same as the rest of you."

Devon gives my hand a squeeze, kisses my forehead, and says to Charles, "Come on. You and I need to talk. Alone. Fate can introduce your guys." Charles nods and a path clears for him. He puts a hand on my cheek as he walks by. Natasha raises an eyebrow but says nothing. I introduce Benny and Rico to everyone else, Owen, John, and Brad offer to take the boys off to find rooms. Billy introduces me to Ryna and Seamus right before he kisses

Natasha and takes Seamus off with him saying, "They are going to talk and decide things, we don't want to be involved."

Seamus says, "Nice to meet you Fate, I hope we get to see more of each other."

Ryna looks me up and down, "I think we will be friends."

"I would like that. Very much. Now, tell me all the things that have happened since I was taken."

Natasha laughs, "Come on. Let's go to the kitchen where Maria can correct me while she plies us all with food and coffee."

"Oh, yes. Charles' cook was excellent, but he was no Maria."

We all wander off to the kitchen with Ajah and Ryna leading the way. I nudge Natasha and point at the two of them. She smiles and mouths, "Later."

Twenty-Five

I take Charles off to the basement. We have it set up for training, meaning it is magically reinforced and we won't pull the entire building down on top of ourselves. I open the door and motion for him to go first. He eyes me and I grin. He finally shrugs before stepping through the doorway and starting down the stairs. I chuckle as I follow him, closing the door behind me. Vampires and shifters both tend to have an excellent ability to hear. The door and the rest of the room have a sound proofing spell that engages when the door is closed. He waits at the bottom of the stairs; I walk by and lead him to a couple chairs we have down here for resting between sessions.

"Would you like a water? We don't keep much else down here."

Charles declines and we sit. He watches me as I watch him while I try to figure out what to say. I start with, "Are you done seeking revenge on me for something I didn't do anyway?"

"Just going to jump right in with that, huh?" Charles runs a hand across the back of his neck, "I spoke to my father recently. He showed up the same day as Pru, oddly enough. He confessed to being the reason for my mother's death, and Pru pretty well confirmed what he said. In many more words than were absolutely necessary. Yes, I am done with seeking revenge. I apologize for blaming you. For hunting you and for murdering Fate numerous times."

"Thank you. I do appreciate that. We appear to have another problem, though. I am told that you can't let go of Fate? Going to need you to explain some things."

Charles leans forward, elbows on his knees and head in his hands. Lifting his head from his hands, he says, "I don't know how much I can explain. The first time I saw her with you, I was enraged, and it didn't have anything to do with what I thought about you. I wanted to kill the both of you, and I didn't really know why. It frightened me. I left and later sought her out and killed her so that you wouldn't have her. That pattern followed her every incarnation. It was never you that I found first, it was always her. You were how I confirmed that it was definitely her. This time, it was different. I watched her grow up. I have been here the whole time. I studied her and even attended her wedding."

The shock must have shown on my face because Charles nods, "I know. I know. It is twisted and stalker sick, and *I couldn't stay away from her*. When her husband died, I watched her at the funeral. When I let her see me and she waved at me, it was all I could do not to run to her. I contented myself with going to the library and talking to her. When she spoke to me I knew I couldn't let her go and the strangest thing happened, this odd… fog? It lifted away from me, and Fate was even more of a draw. Over the past few weeks, the pull I feel toward her has only gotten stronger. Which was why I kidnapped her. Part of the way she convinced me to bring her back was to say that she wouldn't banish me from her life."

I reach out and give his shoulder a squeeze. "I do understand. I felt the same way every time she died. I needed to find her immediately. It was as though part of my soul was held away from me and it hurt the entire time. I was actively avoiding her this time while staying as close as I could, imagine my surprise when I found her in the library. I should have expected it though. She loved books, and she chose to be the Chronicler for the witches. A library is exactly where she would end up. Maybe subconsciously I was hoping to run into her. What I need to know now is, are you going to try to keep her away from me? From the rest of her family? What are your intentions?"

"I need to be in her life. I told her that I would not interfere in your relationship," Charles grins, "though I am available should she tire of you. I am not going to keep her away from anyone. I will follow her to the ends of the earth. I want to keep her safe from the woman that her husband hired to kill her. Honestly, I would take whatever she will allow me."

Studying him, I wonder what magic has brought him to this point, or is it perhaps that some other magic kept him from it for so long? "I will follow her lead in most things. However, I will hunt you down and turn you to ash should you try to take her from me again. It won't matter what she requests at that point, one kidnapping more is all it will take to end your life. Are we clear on that?"

Charles smirks at me, "Then why didn't you come take her from me all this time?"

I lean forward, putting my face mere inches from his, "Because she begged me not to, we found you and could have taken her from you. She believed you were good and would return her. We gave her the chance to prove that. Even still, she was running out of time. We would have come to take her from you tonight if she had not been returned to us." Sitting back it is my turn to smirk as the connotations of what I said sink in and Charles grows pale with the knowledge that he would never have seen her again if we had come to take her back.

Swallowing, Charles says, "I suppose that does put a different light on things. We were clear before, but now I am crystal clear on what the risks are and I can't lose contact with Fate. Congratulations, you found the weakness I didn't know I had until recently."

In the kitchen upstairs…

I know there are questions a plenty to be asked, I feel lucky that Memré isn't here to get in on the grilling. "Where is Memré?"

Natasha chuckles, "Well, she is out on a date. Her mother set up a date for her and said if she went out on this one date, she wouldn't bother her about it for a year. So she is out on a date with a guy her age that her mother picked. She said it was a win-win situation. If she likes the guy, then great, found a guy she likes. If not, then it was one wasted evening for the quiet of an entire year of her mom not hounding her to find someone."

I nod as Maria sets a hot plate of cheesy enchiladas in front of me, "Thanks Maria, I missed your food. His cook does not compare to you. We are so blessed that you are willing to work here."

She pats my face, "We missed you too. Now eat." With an extra hard pat, she turns away and heads back for the stove. I watch her for a minute, her movements seem a little more jerky than usual and she is taking great care to keep her face away from us as she starts pulling things out to bake. Did we luck the fuck out and hire an outstanding woman to cook and manage the house that bakes her feelings? Oh man, she is getting all the gifts.

Natasha clears her throat and I leave off from watching Maria. Looking at Natasha as she says, "Now that you are home, care to explain the pull you felt? To Charles, that is? Or what is happening with Pru? Is she ok?"

Between bites and questions, I get the entire story of the goings on with Pru while I was at Charles' house. All the way to now, where we have Pru sedated into a coma for our protection as well as her own, both to allow her brain some time to heal and to give us time to find an ethical, powerful, mind witch that specializes in healing.

Ryna's eyes go big, "Your work as Chronicler should help you in that respect. But I don't know if even that will suffice, what you seek is just so rare. Is there a doctor tending to her?"

"Yes, Doctor Z is who suggested this after she knocked him out and came downstairs to antagonize me some more. He does know some that he said may be talented enough. He also suggested I search."

"Fascinating. I thought the mind talents were becoming more rare, perhaps I have only been moving in the wrong circles to see them."

"I can't speak for all witches, but until recently I was under the impression that becoming a vampire would be the end of my time as a witch. I know some vampires believe that as well. Perhaps they hide from vampire kind because they fear the loss of an ability so integral to the healing work they do?"

Natasha chimes in at this point, "I think Fate may have the right of it. I mingled with everyone because of Grams, so I knew much earlier on that it wouldn't. But we don't talk about it really, after we are grown. Even when I told my friends about hot vampire sex, nobody asked if I was worried about losing my powers if they turned me. It's just an unspoken thing, sort of like marrying the good guy generally means you are getting fooled."

I narrow my eyes at Natasha, "Way to call me out there." We both laugh and she shrugs.

Ryna looks disturbed, "I think it is very good that you are working to start your foundation and the library. I think I would like to contribute to your book on vampire lore. I think there are things that maybe the men will not know or perhaps just do not consider important. Similar to the knowledge of where the clitoris is, it is very important but many men do not seem to understand this and so they ignore it."

Ajah is laughing before Ryna ever finishes her speech and by the time she does finish Natasha and I are laughing as well. Ryna joins in, whether from amusement at her own cleverness or because she found it funny after the words came out of her mouth. Either way she is laughing too. I see Maria holding on to the counter at the far end of the kitchen and her stomach as she leans over laughing.

Just as we start to calm down Natasha says, "I hear the basement door opening, I think they are on their way back up."

Twenty-Six

FATE

We listen as they come up the stairs; they aren't talking so we can't gauge the mood between them and that causes some apprehension. Fighting vampires are just terrible for a house. We all watch as they walk into the kitchen and over to where I am sitting. I turn to face them on my barstool. They both stand there staring at me like they don't have a brain between them until I can't stand it anymore and say, "So? Did you work it out or what?"

They both start laughing and I breathe a sigh of relief. Devon says, "Yes, we worked things out between us. It would seem he is nearly as devoted to you as I am at this point."

I am overly thrilled at this and I jump up, grabbing the two of them in a big hug.

As I get my arms on the two of them, a resounding BOOM echoes through the house and I freeze with the two of them locked in my arms. They throw their arms around me and shift their bodies so I am now between them, shielded from whatever made the noise but awkwardly positioned.

Someone clears their throat and Natasha says, "Who the fuck are you and what are you doing here?"

I drop to a crouch, spin and stand with a step forward to keep from being dragged back into the shelter of the guy's arms, entirely too much distraction there. Looking across the kitchen, I see a man standing there, flames in his dark hair. His skin is the color of bronze with a blue tint to it, and he is wearing black leather pants under a black t-shirt with an AC/DC logo emblazoned across it. I feel Devon and Charles step up next to me, one on either side.

The man has been looking at each of us while I studied him. His eyes stop when they reach me. A smile lights his face as he says, "Fate, you are as lovely as your mother. She will be here shortly. I am so glad you finally got those two idiots together. I began to think it would never happen, one constantly trying to murder you and the other failing to stop it every time. I thought being vampires would help them to protect you, but nooo. We had to pick dumb and dumber to protect you."

We all watch and listen in fascination as this stranger goes on and on about Devon and Charles being too dumb to protect me and how many times they have thought about replacing them when a portal of light opens up a couple feet away from him and he says, "Ah, here she is! Hello my love." A gorgeous woman with white hair and skin of blued alabaster steps through the portal wearing a flowing dress of midnight blue and it closes behind her as she greets the man in our kitchen saying, "Oh love, I so look forward to our time together. Soon. Soon. For now," she turns and begins walking toward me, "hello my darling daughter and her two idiots. I am so sorry I cannot stay for long, I must get back to serve my time at mother's house. Hekate is covering for me, but even still, I haven't long."

She reaches out and draws me into her arms, hugging me to her and it feels so nice. This is how mothers should hug. Is it possible this gorgeous woman could be my mother? Where has she been all this time? Releasing me, she places her hands on my shoulders and looks me in the eyes, "I am your mother. I hate it that I haven't been with you all this time. Your father," she gestures with one hand at the man still standing in my kitchen, "will have more time to answer questions. For now, all I can do is to be present for the ceremony to unlock your goddess-hood." She turns to look at the man, "Come over here dear, we need to get this done so I can get back." He crosses the kitchen to stand next to her. She keeps a hand on one of my shoulders while he places a hand on my other shoulder. Standing side by side, they begin to glow as they chant:

Heavy lies the weight of power
    Even as it first flowers.
    We unlock that which lies within,
    Your destiny now to begin.

Something inside me pops, and I feel a rush of power. They stop glowing as the chant ends. She reaches out and circles her arms around me once again, "I love you more than just about anything, my darling daughter. I will come see you again when my sentence is over for the year. Be safe and trust your instincts, they will not lead you astray." With that, she releases me from the shelter of her arms and darts across the room into the portal that has reopened. We can hear, faintly, a voice yelling "Kore" coming from the other side of the portal. It closes behind her, leaving the kitchen a little emptier.

Twenty-Seven

FATE

The guy that arrived with the loud noise and leather pants is still standing here watching me so I take the opportunity given me and ask, "Who exactly are you, anyway? Who is she? I assume she has a name beyond her being my mother?"

He smiles, "Oh little princess, you should sit down for this." I make no move to sit and he raises an eyebrow at me but continues, "I am your father, known by everyone else as Hades, god of the Underworld. Your mother is Persephone, goddess of spring, renewal, and the Underworld."

I am a little floored by this, but I am made of sterner stuff than to fall out over this news. Besides, this just leaves me with a lot more questions. "I am willing to take you both being my parents on faith for now, especially since you have the flame thing." Charles chokes back a laugh behind me, "But I have questions. So many questions. To start with, why did you both give me up? Are you going to stay and answer them, since she had somewhere to be? Where did she go? Why couldn't she stay and talk to me?"

Hades pops a chair into existence and has a seat, "Yes, I can stay and answer questions. Now that you have your goddess-hood activated, you'll need training anyway or you are likely to accidentally blow out the side of your house here. Would you care to sit while we talk, or shall I spend my time craning my neck to look up at you?"

Devon and Charles bring a chair in for me just then, setting it down just behind me while everyone else in the kitchen perches themselves on a barstool, except for Charles and Devon who have left and brought back their own chairs that they set down flanking me.

Hades waits calmly, watching me the entire time, like he is starved for the sight of me. Once they have seated themselves he speaks, "I will start with the question of why we gave you up. We had no choice, it was the only way we could see to keep you alive long enough to activate your goddess-hood before Demeter's sentence ended and she came hunting you. Though that did not go as planned since the two we sent to guard you have been incredibly incompetent at their job." He glares at Charles and Devon in turn before looking back to Charles, "You especially! I can't believe you killed her so many times! What were you thinking? Idiot!"

Charles doesn't even look annoyed by this, if anything he looks pained at the reminder. Charles looks to Hades, "I don't know. Every time I saw her in the past I was enraged, immediately. This time I," he glances my way and licks his lips, "I watched her grow up this time. I have been here nearly as long as she has and this time, for what-ever reason, the rage wasn't there. But the need to stay near her was. When I finally got close enough for her to speak to me, it was like a fog was lifted as soon as I heard her voice."

Hades brow has scrunched down as Charles spoke. He looks ferocious as he says, "That is unusual. Considering as you two have been attached to her since she was born," brows raise and cries of what and how interrupt his speech. He narrows his eyes at us, "You can speak or I can speak, pick one."

I swallow, "You, please, continue."

"Where was I? Oh, yes, you two were spirits hating the halls of my home in the Underworld when she was born the first time. As soon as you saw her, that was it. You followed her everywhere. When we were forced to make the choice to send her away to grow up anonymous and safer than was possible with us. You two were determined to stay with her wherever she went, so we sent you back in your own bodies."

I nod, "That makes sense and helps me understand why I am drawn to both of them. I still don't understand why you had to send me away. What made your home so dangerous for me?"

Hades grimaces, "That we can lay at Demeter's feet. She was constantly trying to kidnap you and planned to do terrible things to you. She is very sick. We have theories about it being caused by her boyfriend. Your mother has never been able to name him, she only calls him the beast. From what we know, he wants to plant his soul in the body of a god or goddess, he isn't picky. They were working to do this to your mother, and still would were Hekate not with her when she serves her time visiting her mother."

"Wait, what? Serves her time visiting her mother? Her mom is Demeter and tried to take her body from her for the use of someone else and she still has to visit her? What asshole decided that?"

Hades starts laughing loudly, curling up in the chair he is laughing so hard. He looks up and says, "Do you hear that, brother? She wants to know what asshole decided that!" Thunder claps loudly over the house and Hades laughs harder before he looks up again and says, "Get over yourself. You could have ended this sentence centuries ago, but chose to keep it going. This is just one of the many consequences of your actions."

Looking back at us he says, "In case you were unable to interpret that answer, Zeus is the one that made that decision. He made a rule that parents could demand their children visit them regularly, no matter their age in order to ensure that they were not plotting against them. He did it out of an abundance of caution since overthrowing his father was how he came to power. He forgets that he couldn't have done that without the help of his mother. I have always thought that instead of keeping a watchful eye on some possible rebellion, it would be better to treat his wife and children well. But that is neither here nor there. The rule stands, and so your mother must visit with her mother every summer. Every summer Hekate goes with her. They watch each other's backs and work to come home safe."

"That is horrible. I think I understand why you gave me away, but Devon mentioned recently that every life he has met me in I was an orphan or adopted. I don't understand how that happened?"

"Ah, well, your mother is the smartest, most cunning person I have ever met. She knew she didn't want you going through the recycle process, and so she cursed herself and you. Every time you die, she is immediately pregnant with you again. That kept you coming back to her, and I arranged for the boys to become vampires so that they would always be there waiting for you. Though your mother is the one that sealed the connection between the three of you after she talked to the Fates. I don't know what they said, but after that she wouldn't hear of the two of you not being bound to Fate."

"I knew I was bound to Devon. You mean there is a bond to Charles as well? I'm not just a terrible person?"

Hades chuckles, "Two things here. One, it doesn't make you a terrible person to have more than one partner unless you are shady about it. As long as everyone is an adult and consented to it, it is fine. Second, yes, there is a bond between all of you. However, on your end it is a different thing. See, these two were adults when the bond was created. So, until you choose to create the bond with one or both of them, it is one sided. That is why you have the bond with Devon now, but only feel the pull of the other possible bond. You can choose to cement the bond or deny it, if you deny it Charles will be freed of it as well. Being freed of the bond will not, however, erase any feelings he developed for you. Nor any you developed for him. It just means that the two of you would not feel a continual need to be around the other. No rush, take your time deciding. I can tell you how to do it, now that you are a goddess in your own right."

I know my eyes must be a little bugged out, I can see the guys struggling to maintain their poker faces in my peripheral vision. I feel like I need some time to absorb all this and I know I need some time to talk to my father alone, without even Devon. I look at Devon and ask, "Would you be terribly offended if I ask you all to give me some time alone with my father?" I look around to Charles and everyone else, "I love you all, but I would really appreciate some time alone with my father if you don't mind."

Natasha, Ajah, Ryna, and Maria nod and file out of the kitchen. Charles places his hand on mine and gives it a squeeze, "I need to make this guy find me a room, anyway." He stands, tips his head at Hades, "Nice to meet you, sir. Hope we can meet under better circumstances in the future."

Hades nods at him and turns to watch Devon. Devon leans over, kisses my cheek and then stands, "It was a pleasure to finally meet you, sir. Have a good night." The two of them leave the room discussing where exactly Charles will be sleeping.

After I watch them leave I turn back to my father, "What do I call you? I mean, should I call you both by name or the formal mother and father? Mom and Dad? Is there something else you would prefer to go by?"

Hades swallows, "I would really like it if you called me Dad, and I know your mother is dying to hear you call her Mom. She has been waiting all your lives for that moment."

I nod, "Ok, Dad, wow, that is so cool to say. It was mother and father with my adopted parents. I hope I will be able to spend more time getting to know both of you?"

"Yes, of course. We don't have to stay away now that you are grown and your goddess-hood is activated. Those that are fully gods or goddesses, their god-powers do not activate while they are still maturing. Well, not anymore. That was put in place after certain ones of us wreaked havoc with those abilities. So we implemented some safe-guards. We only stayed away to keep Demeter from finding you. Unless you don't want us to be a part of your life, we are here. We will be part of your life from now on. We never wanted to stay away from you, doing so while knowing where you were has been difficult for both of us.

We have had others monitor you, but that isn't the same as being there, playing an active role as your parents. We couldn't even help when we knew things were going badly." Hades runs a hand through his hair, making the flames dance wildly for a moment.

"So you are where I got the flames from. Do you have control over them or do they do as they will?"

He laughs, "I have some control over them. They are connected to my emotions so if I am angry they flare up, happy they dance all over… They don't hurt anyone unless I am being hurt. It does work a little like a protection device in that way." Hades tips his head and seems to be listening to something. "I have to go. A special case has arrived in the Underworld and I am needed. Would you mind it terribly if I came back to see you soon? Or you could come see me?"

"I could? That would be amazing. How do I do that?"

"You are from the Underworld, now that you are acti-vated all you need to do is focus on being there and you will be." He stands, "May I have a hug before I go?"

"Yes!" I stand and throw my arms around my Dad for the first time. He smells of night air and fire, hugging him feels a bit like coming home. I always wondered what it would be like to hug a dad that loved me, and would I be able to tell the difference? Now I know the answer is yes. A hug doesn't lie. Lips might, hips can send a message you didn't intend, but hugs never lie. I release him so he can get to work, and I see a tear tracking its way down his face.

He brushes it away saying, "It has been so long since I held my little girl. I am so glad to be able to see you again. If you don't come see me, I will be back in a few days. I love you Fate."

He disappears as I tell him that I love him too. I sit back down to collect myself; it feels like my whole heart is in my throat. I breathe deeply to calm myself. I want to try going to the Underworld now, but if I leave without saying anything, the guys are going to lose their minds. I content myself with the knowledge that I can and will, but now I need to find out where Charles and Devon decided that Charles would sleep after finding out that he could be a bond mate for me as well.

Author's Note

Reviews really help other people decide whether or not to read a book. If you feel a way about this book, I would sincerely appreciate a review.

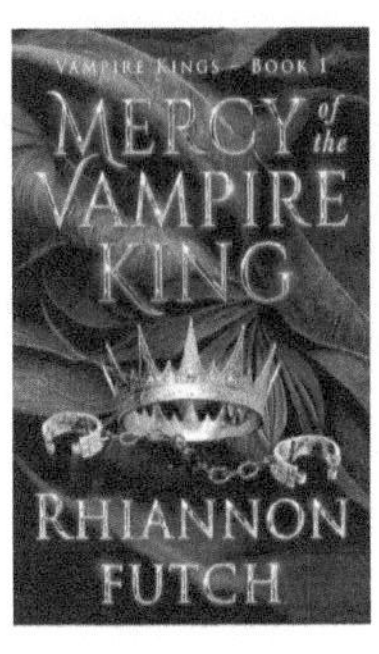

What kind of fool would beg mercy from a vampire, even if he is a king?

Valdís

I have one hope to keep my title, lands, and the people we are supposed to take care of out of the hands of my mother and sister. I must beg the vampire kings to grant me aid and just hope they aren't hungry as people that annoy them have a way of disappearing. Arriving at the castle, I realize I am in way over my head when the scent of the king lights a fire in my soul that could get me killed.

Knox

King of a land that is nothing more than a myth to the rest of the world, I just want my time in charge to pass quickly. Until she arrives, begging so sweetly. Her blood sings to mine and her attitude promises anything but the monotony of late. What seemed like nothing more than a family dispute over inheritance becomes more when they try to take all our lives.

War

My quest to save my people revealed worlds of treachery, and now the Outsiders are back. Once again, looking to take our country. The king may have mercy on my people but at what cost?

Mercy of the Vampire King *is the first in the completed Vampire Kings series. For fans of Geneva Lee or Katee Robert, this is a steamy, paranormal romance with a happily ever after at the end of the series.*

A Free Story for You!

Enjoyed A Vampire's Fate? Not ready to quit reading yet? If you sign up for my newsletter at

this page , where you will receive Fated for Halloween, the origin story of Fate's Chronicles, right away as my thank you gift for choosing to hang out with me.

Or, how Fate's Chronicles began.

I like to think I was a happy Goddess, even when my mother was incredibly tiresome. All that changed when the Beast showed up on our doorstep. Escaping the confines of the house and the terrible way the Beast looks at me I find a dark stranger sunbathing naked in my field.

The violence within...

He is trying to kill me. I want to believe my mother

will protect me but my dark stranger feels safer than this home or my mother ever have. I have to make a choice soon, or my life will be ended before it has really begun.

Whoever I choose, my life will never be the same again.

Fated for Halloween preview

Kore yelled toward the interior of the house from near the front door, "Mother, I'm off to my field, I feel a need to be outside with my thoughts. I'll return soon."

"Waaaaaiiiiitttt!!!"

Kore rolled her eyes, she knew she shouldn't have even hoped she could get away so easily she listens as her mother runs to intercept her before she leaves the house. As if she were going somewhere her mother couldn't find her. Or that was even off the property.

Huffing and puffing Demeter rounded the corner at full speed with her head tucked down. Kore could see that she would not be able to stop in time as she hadn't yet realized she was in the entryway. Kore neatly stepped to the left before her mother could plow into her, leaving Demeter to hit the wall in front of her. It didn't seem to faze her though it did stop her. She turned around searching until her eyes light upon her most coveted child, Kore. For her part Kore waited patiently for her mother to gather her wits and try to force her to stay in the house under her stifling presence. Demeter draws in, uncomfortably close to her daughter, placing a hand on her shoulder and speaking directly into her face, "Oh sweet girl, why would you want to go out there? It's all bugs and muggy heat. You should stay here in the house where it is lovely and cool. What if some man crosses your path? He could do terrible things to your reputation!"

Kore's eyes move toward the ceiling of their own volition, "Mother, please. What do I care if some man hinges my reputation on whether or not I have been in the company of other men? Because I have been in the company of men, Beltane is my holiday. My favorite time of the year and I take at least one lover every year at the fires. My reputation is that I am the Goddess of Spring and New Beginnings, not some spinster. I am grown mother. I live here simply to humor you. I will not become a prisoner of your house."

Demeter grabbed her heart with one hand and the wall with the other, "My heart, oh my heart, why don't you just rip it out already? My own daughter treats me like this! No Goddess of the Harvest and Seasons ever had a daughter so ungrateful!"

Foot tapping Kore says, "I am going mother. Are you quite finished?"

Peering up through her lashes to see that Kore isn't falling for it at all Demeter straightened up, having decided to take a different tack, "Fine. You don't care about your mother, the least you could is take your maidens with you. You'll want to be married one day and you'll thank me then. Take the maidens if you must go."

"Fine. If that will stop your harping, tell them to come. Now will you go back to whatever it was that you were doing?"

Demeter bellowed into the house, "Girls! Come escort my daughter!" Turning back to Kore she says, "No, I can't go back to what I was doing as now I must lay down, sick with worry that you might be ravished while you wander like a thoughtless child."

"You know, I have always loved a good ravishing, you probably shouldn't worry about that mother."

"Impudent child!"

"I am over a century old mother, childhood is long gone."

The maidens Demeter summoned arrived and Kore opened the door, they filed out with her following the last one out the door. Kore left the door standing open because she knew it would irritate her mother. The women followed the path through the woods surrounding the house, emerging out into a bright field that extends as far as the eye can see. Kore looks at the maidens, "Let's all lay down in this soft grass to enjoy the rays of this glorious sun." The maidens, her mother's little spies, agreed and picked a spot fluffy with clover. Kore laid down with them, waited for them to grow comfortable and with a wave of her hand sent them all to sleep.

Rising from her spot in the clover Kore shook her head and started walking out into her field. The combination of rolling hills, wild flower filled meadow and bright sunny day did much to improve her dark mood. As she walked she realized there was a dark hole ahead of her that should not be there and decided to investigate. Striding through the field she drew near the cave and was only a few feet away she noticed the body laid bare for all to see in her field.

There, laying in the grass was a gorgeous man. His clothing lay in a pile next to him but they were just clothes and not near so interesting as the hard planes of him. His eyes were closed so Kore let hers roam freely over all that gorgeous exposed flesh. His hair was dark and appeared long, how long she couldn't tell. His face, all strong angles and smooth beard with long lashes that lay against his cheeks, those looked soft as down. His shoulders broad, just the right kind for throwing a body over if he were interested in taking her off to ravish. The very thought caused a flood of moisture in her core. Those well formed shoulders led to an eight pack that looked like a ladder straight to the vee over the patch of dark curls where his shaft rested. It was soft at the moment but still an impressive size and Kore had seen enough members to be a fair judge. His legs were thick and powerful looking, as were his arms. Over all he was very well proportioned and Kore wouldn't mind a more prolonged and active visit with him.

"If you've had your eyeful, why not have a lie down in this gorgeous sun?"

"Oh! I didn't realize you were awake. My apologies, I should have called out. Though you are in my field."

"I don't mind. Have your fill of looking, but the sun really is very nice. You might give sunbathing a go. I have it on very good authority that today will continue to be a very nice day. Go ahead, I won't peek and I can assure you I will not ravish you."

Kore dropped her clothing during his little speech and is laying down when he finishes. She laughs, "Well, that is disappointing. I love a good ravishing." Turning her head she watched as he grimaces.

Lips still twisted and never opening his eyes he said, "You are probably completely inexperienced and vanilla is not my favorite flavor, nor am I interested in teaching anyone."

Kore's laughter rang thru the field, "What? Oh my, no." She rolled to her side and propped her head on her hand, "I hate to be the one to destroy your illusion of having been found by a fair maid with no experience to speak of, but I am not her. I am the Goddess of Spring and new beginnings, my whole season is about having as much sex as possible. Frankly, I am what hunts the hunters in the woods. Mother hates it, which is why she has taken to sending maidens out with me. But I just put them to sleep.

And Beltane! Beltane is my holy day, it infuriates mother that she cannot stop my attendance at the fires."

One of his eyes opens, "OH really?" She watched as his eye roamed her body.

"Yes, really. My time out is limited before mother comes hunting me and finds her maidens at the edge of the field. Care for a tryst in the sun before I must leave?"

His cock twitched when she said tryst, making her grin. Both his eyes are open now taking in her form and finally meeting her eyes, "Are you quite sure that you would want to tryst with one so mired in the Underworld as I?" He sits up, waving his hand at the cave and his appearance is darker, blue fire seeming to play at the tips of his hair. His dark eyes are soul deep, Kore could get lost in there. His darkness doesn't frighten her, no, it calls the darkness in her.

She noted the surprise on his face as she leans toward him and ever so gently touches her lips to his and whispers, "More than anything I have ever wanted in my entire long life. Your darkness feeds my starving soul."

Kore drew back, put enough space between them that she could see his eyes as she brought a hand up to his face, and caressed his cheek. His eyes drifted shut as he leaned in to the softness of her hand. She trailed her hand down the column of his neck and across his chest then traced the lines of his abs as his breath grew ragged. His hand shots out and grabbed hers before she could reach the goal that strained toward her wandering hand.

"Before we go any farther princess, beware that being

with me might taint your pretty little soul in a way those hunters and Beltane fire lovers cannot."

Kore laughed and dropped the control that kept the rest of her nature hidden from people like her mother. The meadow darkened though the day remained bright. Kore's pale blue eyes darkened to a color more indigo and her pale skin becomes bluish, her hair going from blond to white and seeming to float in its own breeze.

Hades had never seen anything so beautiful as Kore without her mask of innocence, he could live in her shadow if only he would be allowed to gaze upon her. Lucky for him it appeared that she wanted more than for him to live in her shadow.

Kore tugged her hand from his grip and used it to urge him to lie back down as she crawled over top him.

***

Hours later the two lie spent in the grass, Kore realizes the sun has nearly left the sky. "I must go back now, the maidens will be waking soon and I need to be there when they do." Sitting up she reached for her clothing and began dressing.

Hades also sat up, "I should probably go tend the Underworld, send some souls where they belong. Do you have a name other than princess?"

Giggling as she slipped her dress over her head she said, "Of course I do. My name is Kore. Do you have a name dark man of the Underworld?"

"I am Hades. You could say I am *the* dark man of the underworld. Will you come see me again?" He asks as he reached for her hand and used it to tug her closer before he wrapped his arms around her.

"I can't get away often. I would like to see you again. How will I get word to you when I can sneak away? Surely now that you know my name you know as well, Hades, the reputation of my mother in regard to me. The same as I know of your reputation as the dark lord of the Underworld, ruthless and evil as they come."

"That doesn't bother you?"

Snuggled into his chest she said, "No, not a bit. This has been the best afternoon I have spent in many years. Now, how will I contact you? I really must get going. They will wake when the sun touches the horizon."

Hades pulls a black feather from a pocket of his drape, "When you would have me pull out this feather and hold it in your hand. Bring it to your lips and blow on it. I will arrive here presently."

She took the feather from his hand and slipped it into a hidden pocket within her dress. A quick kiss pressed to his lips, Kore stood and took off running, yelling goodbye over her shoulder as she went. Looking toward the sun Hades saw that it is no more than an inch above the horizon.

Kore made it back to the maidens and lay down just a bare breath before they woke up. Pretending to wake up with them Kore stood and dusted the grass off her clothing,

"Let us go back to the house, mother will be worried. We have slept the afternoon away in the sun."

Fated for Halloween is only available by subscribing to my once monthly newsletter at:

https://www.subscribepage.com/r4v6m2

Rhiannon writes steamy paranormal romance. She is an avid reader of many authors in a variety of genre though she tends more toward paranormal.

She has three former pound puppies that she dotes on and three daughters that she adores.

Rhiannon has lived in multiple states though she is currently residing in North Carolina. Wandering, witching, and reading with her puppies and husband are what she does when she isn't writing.

To learn about what is happening in Rhiannon's world and get loads of pupper cuteness, sign up for the by using the QR code below to visit my website.

Also by Rhiannon Futch

The Daughter of the Moon series-

<u>Selena Rose, Daughter of the Moon Book 1</u>

<u>Thorns of the Rose, Daughter of the Moon Book 2</u>

<u>Heart of the Rose, Daughter of the Moon Book 3</u>

The Fate's Chronicles series

<u>A Vampire's Fate</u>

<u>A Vampire's Treasure</u>

<u>A Vampire's Dream</u>

<u>A Vampire's Chase</u>

<u>A Vampire's Fight</u>

<u>Fated for Halloween -</u> only available via email signup

The Belancore Witches of North Carolina series

<u>Witchy Ever After</u>

<u>A Witchy New Year</u>

<u>My Witchy Valentine</u>

Sin series

<u>Sin on a Dark Knight</u>

<u>Sin on a Broken Heart</u>

<u>Sin on a Burning Heart</u>

Sin on a Vengeful Heart

The Vampire Kings Series

Mercy of the Vampire King

Shame of the Vampire King

Pursuit of the Vampire King

Prey of the Vampire King

Reign of the Vampire King

Coming Soon

Love and Vampires Series

Olivia's Fall

Olivia's Prison

Olivia's Flight

Olivia's Family

Warriors of the Old Gods

A Dream of Blood

A Dream of Wolves

A Dream of Stone

A Dream of Ravens

A Dream of Bones